TALE TELLER

Wisdom For The Journey

100 Inspirational Short Stories For Adults

This book was professionally typeset on Reedsy.
Find out more at reedsy.com

Contents

1   Introduction   1

2   The Path of Purpose: Discovering Your
Life's Meaning and...   3

3   The Mountain of Wisdom: Reaching
Greater Understanding...   5

4   The Circle of Self-Care: Prioritizing
Your Well-Being and...   8

5   The Forest of Creativity: Nurturing
Innovation and...   11

6   The Dance of Confidence: Expressing
Self-Assurance and...   14

7   The Ocean of Empathy: Connecting
with Others Through...   16

8   The Bridge of Forgiveness: Crossing
Over to Peace and...   19

9   The River of Gratitude: Flowing with
Thankfulness and...   21

10   The Path of Authenticity: Embracing
Your True Self and...   24

11   The Garden of Resilience: Growing
Stronger Through Adversity   26

12   The Garden of Courage: Cultivating
Bravery and Overcoming...   28

13 The Bridge of Resilience: Crossing Over to Strength and...   30

14 The Forest of Reflection: Finding Inner Clarity and Insight...   33

15 The Circle of Empowerment: Supporting Others and Encouraging...   36

16 The Ocean of Hope: Finding Optimism and Possibility in the...   39

17 The Path of Growth: Navigating Challenges and Embracing...   41

18 The Dance of Authenticity: Expressing Your True Self and...   43

19 The Mountain of Perseverance: Climbing Higher Through...   46

20 The River of Graciousness: Flowing with Grace and Compassion...   49

21 The Circle of Inspiration: Sparking Creativity and Passion...   52

22 The Path of Resilient Love: Overcoming Obstacles and...   55

23 The Forest of Renewal: Rejuvenating Your Spirit and...   57

24 The Ocean of Forgiveness: Letting Go of Grudges and Finding...   59

25 The Mountain of Transformation: Reimagining Your Life...   61

26 The Circle of Gratitude: Fostering a Heart of Thankfulness...   63

27 The Bridge of Acceptance: Embracing Yourself and Others with...   65

28 The Dance of Liberation: Breaking Free
    from Limitations and...   68
29 The Garden of Mindfulness: Cultivat-
    ing Peace and Clarity...   71
30 The Path of Courageous Vulnerability:
    Embracing Authenticity...   74
31 The River of Harmony: Finding Bal-
    ance and Unity Amidst...   77
32 The Garden of Resilient Joy: Cultivat-
    ing Happiness and...   80
33 The Path of Radical Acceptance: Em-
    bracing Imperfection and...   82
34 The Circle of Authentic Connection:
    Building Meaningful...   85
35 The Ocean of Compassionate Action:
    Making a Positive...   88
36 The Bridge of Self-Compassion: Learn-
    ing to Treat Yourself...   91
37 The Mountain of Self-Discovery: Find-
    ing Your True Self...   94
38 The Forest of Creative Healing: Using
    Art and Imagination to...   97
39 The Circle of Gracious Accountability:
    Taking Responsibility...   99
40 The River of Mindful Communication:
    Building Stronger...   102
41 The Path of Transformative Growth:
    Embracing Change and...   105
42 The Garden of Compassionate Self-
    Reflection: Learning to...   108

43 The Ocean of Empowered Action: Harnessing Your Strength and...   111

44 The Mountain of Fearless Adventure: Conquering Doubt and...   114

45 The Circle of Authentic Expression: Sharing Your Unique...   117

46 The River of Grateful Giving: Cultivating Generosity and...   120

47 The Bridge of Intentional Living: Living with Purpose and...   123

48 The Forest of Mindful Resilience: Strengthening Your Inner...   126

49 The Path of Radiant Positivity: Choosing Joy and Spreading...   129

50 The Circle of Joyful Connection: Building Supportive and...   132

51 The Garden of Mindful Leadership: Inspiring and Empowering...   134

52 The Path of Grateful Abundance: Seeing the Beauty in Life's...   137

53 The Circle of Fearless Vulnerability: Embracing the Unknown...   140

54 The River of Mindful Parenting: Raising Children with...   143

55 The Garden of Mindful Eating: Nourishing Your Body and Soul...   145

56 The Mountain of Unconditional Love: Embracing and Accepting...   148

57 The Path of Empowered Self-Care: Prioritizing Your...   151

58 The Ocean of Limitless Possibilities: Embracing Your Inner...   154

59 The Bridge of Resilient Forgiveness: Letting Go of Grudges...   157

60 The Circle of Courageous Authenticity: Embracing Your True...   160

61 The Forest of Mindful Boundaries: Creating Healthy...   163

62 The Mountain of Relentless Perseverance: Overcoming...   166

63 The Path of Courageous Vulnerability: Authenticity as a Path...   169

64 The Ocean of Compassionate Service: Making a Difference...   172

65 The Circle of Mindful Gratitude: Cultivating Appreciation...   175

66 The Forest of Creative Flow: Tapping into Your Inner...   178

67 The Bridge of Conscious Communication: Using Words Wisely to...   181

68 The River of Resilient Hope: Finding Strength in the Face of...   184

69 The Garden of Intentional Relationships: Nurturing...   187

70 The Mountain of Empowered Boundaries: Saying No with Grace...   190

71 The Garden of Inner Peace: Finding Calm Amidst the Chaos   192

72 The Circle of Radical Acceptance: Embracing Life's...   194

73 The Forest of Self-Discovery: Finding Purpose and Passion...   197

74 The Bridge of Empathetic Listening: Understanding Others...   200

75 The Path of Mindful Healing: Nurturing Your Body and Soul...   203

76 The Ocean of Abundant Joy: Cultivating Happiness and...   206

77 The Mountain of Fearless Exploration: Stepping Out of Your...   209

78 The Circle of Resilient Optimism: Choosing Positivity and...   211

79 The Garden of Authentic Expression: Honoring Your Truth and...   213

80 The River of Mindful Creativity: Tapping into Your Creative...   216

81 The Path of Gracious Humility: Balancing Confidence and...   219

82 The Ocean of Endless Possibilities: Embracing Uncertainty...   221

83 The Mountain of Radical Self-Love: Honoring Yourself and...   223

84 The Garden of Compassionate Communication: Building Bridges...   225

85 The Path of Intentional Living: Creating a Life of Meaning...   228

86 The Circle of Resilient Connection: Navigating Loneliness...   231

87 The Forest of Mindful Self-Compassion: Embracing Your...   234

88 The Bridge of Forgiveness and Recon-
    ciliation: Finding...   237
89 The River of Abundant Creativity: Un-
    leashing Your Creative...   240
90 The Garden of Authentic Gratitude:
    Cultivating a Grateful...   242
91 The Path of Mindful Leadership: Inspir-
    ing and Empowering...   245
92 Conclusion & Free Gift   248

1

Introduction

Welcome to "Wisdom For The Journey: 100 Inspirational Short Stories For Adults". This book is a collection of 100 short stories, each one designed to inspire and uplift readers on their journey through life.

As adults, we face a variety of challenges and obstacles on our paths. It is easy to become bogged down in the day-to-day struggles and forget the beauty and wonder that surrounds us.

This book is intended to serve as a reminder of the richness of life and to help readers find the inspiration they need to keep moving forward with purpose and passion.

Each story in this collection has been carefully selected to offer a unique perspective on the human experience. Some stories may resonate with readers on a personal level, while others may provide a new and unexpected way of looking at the world.

Through these tales, readers will be encouraged to reflect on their own lives, their hopes and dreams, and the people and experiences that have shaped them.

Whether you are in need of a little inspiration, seeking a new perspective, or simply looking for a moment of reflection, "Wisdom For The Journey" offers something for everyone.

I hope that the stories in this book will serve as a source of comfort, guidance, and inspiration, helping you to find the wisdom you need to navigate life's ups and downs with grace and ease.

Positive reviews from wonderful customers like you help other book enjoyers feel confident about choosing to get this book too.

Sharing your happy experience will be greatly appreciated!

2

The Path of Purpose: Discovering Your Life's Meaning and Fulfillment

Once upon a time, there was a young man named Koji who was lost and unsure of his purpose in life. He had tried many different jobs and hobbies, but nothing seemed to give him a sense of fulfillment or direction.

One day, while walking through the forest, Koji stumbled upon an old wise man who was sitting on a rock, gazing at the sky. Koji approached him and asked, "Excuse me, sir, but do you know what my purpose in life is?"

The wise man smiled and replied, "That is something only you can discover for yourself, my friend. But I can offer you some guidance."

The wise man explained to Koji that everyone has a unique path and purpose in life, but it's up to each individual to find it. He suggested that Koji take some time to reflect on his passions and values, and to listen to his heart.

Over the next few weeks, Koji took the wise man's advice and spent time meditating and journaling about his interests and goals. He discovered that he had a deep love for animals and a desire to help them.

One day, Koji came across a local animal shelter that was in need of volunteers. He started spending his free time there, helping to care for the animals and giving them love and attention. Koji found that this work brought him a sense of purpose and fulfillment that he had never experienced before.

As he continued to volunteer at the shelter, Koji realized that he wanted to do more to help animals in need. He decided to go back to school to become a veterinarian.

It wasn't an easy journey, and Koji faced many challenges along the way, but he was determined to pursue his passion and fulfill his purpose. After years of hard work and dedication, Koji finally became a licensed veterinarian.

Now, Koji spends each day helping animals in need and bringing comfort to their owners. He feels a deep sense of fulfillment knowing that he is living his purpose and making a positive impact on the world.

Through his journey, Koji learned that finding your purpose is not always easy, but it's worth the effort. By following your heart and pursuing your passions, you can discover the path that is meant for you and live a fulfilling life.

3

The Mountain of Wisdom: Reaching Greater Understanding Through Life's Lessons

Once upon a time, there was a young man who set out on a journey to seek wisdom. He climbed mountains, crossed deserts, and swam across rivers, but still, he felt he had not found what he was looking for.

One day, as he was walking through a dense forest, he came across an old sage who was sitting on a rock, deep in thought. The young man approached him and asked, "Oh wise one, can you share with me the secrets of wisdom?"

The old sage looked at him with a gentle smile and said, "My dear young man, wisdom cannot be taught or learned, it can only be gained through experience. Life is the greatest teacher, and the lessons it offers are the keys to unlocking the door of wisdom."

The young man felt a sense of disappointment. He had hoped for an easy answer, a shortcut to wisdom. But the old sage's words gave him a new perspective. He decided to stay with the sage and learn from his experiences.

Days turned into weeks, and weeks into months. The young man assisted the old sage in his daily chores, and in return, the sage shared his life's experiences with him. He told him about the ups and downs, the victories and defeats, the joys and sorrows, and how he learned from each experience.

One day, the young man felt he had gained enough knowledge and was ready to leave. He went to the old sage and thanked him for all that he had learned. The old sage smiled and said, "Remember, my dear young man, wisdom is not just about knowledge, it's also about applying that knowledge in life. Use what you have learned to make a difference in the world."

The young man left the forest feeling enlightened. He realized that wisdom is not just about acquiring knowledge, it's about applying that knowledge to make a positive impact. He started living his life with purpose, using his experiences to help others and make the world a better place.

Years later, the young man had become a wise old man himself. He looked back at his life's journey and realized that the lessons he had learned had helped him become the person he was today. He remembered the old sage's words and felt grateful for the experience that had transformed his life.

In the end, he knew that the journey to wisdom was not an

easy one, but it was a journey worth taking. He had climbed the mountain of wisdom, and it had been a challenging climb, but the view from the top was worth it. He felt a sense of peace, knowing that he had lived a life of purpose and made a difference in the world.

4

The Circle of Self-Care: Prioritizing Your Well-Being and Finding Inner Balance

Once upon a time, there was a woman named Maya who was always putting others' needs before her own. She worked long hours at a demanding job and spent most of her free time caring for her aging parents and helping her friends whenever they needed it. Despite her endless generosity, Maya often felt exhausted and overwhelmed.

One day, Maya's close friend invited her to a weekend wellness retreat in the mountains. Maya was hesitant at first, feeling guilty about leaving her responsibilities behind, but her friend insisted that she deserved a break. Maya finally relented and agreed to go.

The retreat was held in a beautiful cabin surrounded by lush greenery and a serene lake. The participants spent their days practicing yoga, meditating, and engaging in various self-care activities. For the first time in a long while, Maya felt relaxed and at peace.

As the weekend came to a close, the retreat leader spoke about the importance of self-care and how taking care of oneself is not a selfish act but a necessary one. Maya was struck by these words and realized that she had been neglecting herself for far too long.

When Maya returned home, she decided to make some changes in her life. She started by setting boundaries with her job and dedicating time each day for self-care, whether it be taking a relaxing bath, going for a walk in nature, or simply reading a book. Maya also reached out to her siblings to share the responsibility of taking care of their parents, and they were more than happy to help.

With each day, Maya felt more energized and less stressed. She found that by taking care of herself, she was better equipped to care for those around her. Maya realized that self-care was not selfish but rather essential for her overall well-being.

From then on, Maya made self-care a priority in her life, and her loved ones noticed a positive change in her demeanor. Maya became an advocate for self-care, encouraging others to take care of themselves as well. She learned that by prioritizing her own well-being, she was able to give more to those around her.

In the end, Maya realized that taking care of oneself is not just an act of self-love, but also a necessary component of being able to show up fully for others. She was grateful for the weekend retreat that showed her the importance of self-care and the power it can have in transforming one's life.

5

The Forest of Creativity: Nurturing Innovation and Imagination through Nature

I n the heart of the forest lived a young girl named Emi, who loved nothing more than to explore the woods and all its wonders. Every day, she wandered through the trees, marveling at the birds singing in harmony and the rabbits hopping in unison. The forest was her home, her playground, and her muse.

One day, as she was meandering along the riverbank, Emi stumbled upon a hidden clearing. In the center of the clearing was a grand old tree, its branches reaching high up towards the sky. Emi felt drawn to the tree and decided to take a closer look.

As she approached the tree, Emi noticed a small creature sitting at the base of its trunk. The creature was unlike anything she had ever seen before, with vibrant colors and patterns covering its body. Emi cautiously approached the creature, but it didn't seem to be afraid of her. Instead, it looked up at her with curious eyes.

"Who are you?" Emi asked, fascinated by the creature's beauty.

"I am a forest spirit," the creature replied. "And you, Emi, are a very special girl."

Emi was surprised that the forest spirit knew her name, but she didn't feel afraid. In fact, she felt a sense of calm and comfort in the creature's presence.

The forest spirit continued, "You have a gift, Emi. A gift for creativity and imagination. But sometimes, you doubt yourself and your abilities. You must trust in your own unique talents and embrace your creativity, for it is what makes you truly special."

Emi felt a warmth spreading through her body as she listened to the forest spirit's words. She realized that she had been holding back her creativity, afraid to express herself fully. But now, she felt a sense of freedom and liberation.

From that day on, Emi spent even more time in the forest, drawing inspiration from the trees, animals, and the mysterious forest spirit. She created beautiful art and wrote stories about her adventures in the woods. And she always remembered the forest spirit's wise words, trusting in herself and her creative abilities.

As the years passed, Emi grew into a talented artist and writer, sharing her gifts with the world. And even though she left the forest behind, she never forgot the lessons she learned from the forest spirit. She continued to draw inspiration from nature, and her creativity blossomed even further.

Emi realized that the forest spirit was right – she was a very special girl, with a unique gift to share with the world. And she knew that she would always be grateful for the forest's guidance, and the courage to embrace her creativity with confidence and joy.

6

The Dance of Confidence: Expressing Self-Assurance and Belief in Yourself

There was once a young girl named Maya who loved to dance. She had a natural talent for it and would often dance whenever she had the chance. However, despite her love for dancing, Maya struggled with confidence. She would constantly compare herself to others and feel like she wasn't good enough.

One day, Maya was invited to audition for a prestigious dance school. She was both excited and nervous, as this was a huge opportunity for her. But as she walked into the audition room, she couldn't help but feel intimidated by the other dancers. They all seemed so confident and sure of themselves.

Maya began to doubt herself and her abilities. She started to feel like she wasn't good enough to be there. But then, she remembered something her dance teacher had told her: "Dancing is not about being the best, it's about expressing yourself and enjoying the moment."

With this in mind, Maya took a deep breath and started to dance. She closed her eyes and let the music guide her movements. As she danced, she felt a sense of freedom and joy that she had never experienced before. She stopped worrying about what others might think and just danced for herself.

After the audition, Maya wasn't sure how she did. She didn't know if she was good enough to be accepted into the school. But as she walked out of the building, she realized something. Whether or not she got accepted didn't matter. What mattered was that she had danced with confidence and had given it her all.

A few weeks later, Maya received a letter from the dance school. She opened it anxiously and read the words "Congratulations, you have been accepted!" Maya couldn't believe it. She had made it into the school that she had always dreamed of attending.

From that day on, Maya danced with even more confidence and passion. She realized that confidence wasn't about being the best, but about believing in yourself and your abilities. And as she danced, she inspired others to do the same. Maya learned that confidence isn't something that you have to be born with, but something that you can cultivate and develop over time.

7

The Ocean of Empathy: Connecting with Others Through Understanding and Compassion

Once upon a time, there was a small island in the middle of the ocean. On this island lived a group of people who had everything they needed to survive, but they were not happy. They often quarreled and fought, and no one seemed to understand each other.

One day, a great storm hit the island, and all the people were forced to huddle together for safety. As they waited for the storm to pass, they began to share their stories with each other. They talked about their hopes, dreams, fears, and struggles. For the first time, they listened to each other with empathy and understanding.

When the storm finally passed, something had shifted on the island. The people no longer quarreled and fought. They worked together to repair their homes and rebuild their community. They began to see each other in a new light, not as enemies, but as fellow human beings with their own joys and sorrows.

As time passed, the people of the island continued to practice empathy and understanding. They learned to see things from each other's perspectives, to put themselves in each other's shoes. They discovered that by connecting with each other through empathy, they could build a stronger, more compassionate community.

Years went by, and the island became known as a place of great empathy and understanding. People from all over the world came to visit, hoping to learn from the islanders' example. And the people of the island continued to practice empathy, knowing that it was the key to their happiness and their community's well-being.

One day, an old man was walking along the beach, deep in thought. He had been thinking about all the changes that had happened on the island and how far they had come. Suddenly, he saw a stranger struggling in the water, caught in a strong current. Without hesitation, the old man rushed into the water and pulled the stranger to safety.

As they walked back to the village, the old man asked the stranger why he had come to the island. The stranger replied that he had heard about the island's reputation for empathy and understanding and wanted to experience it for himself.

The old man smiled and said, "You have come to the right place. On this island, we believe that by connecting with others through empathy and understanding, we can make the world a better place."

8

The Bridge of Forgiveness: Crossing Over to Peace and Freedom from Pain

Once upon a time, there was a woman named Lily who had been holding onto a grudge for many years. Her best friend from childhood had betrayed her and caused her a great deal of pain, and she couldn't let go of the anger and resentment that had built up inside of her.

One day, as she was walking along a bridge over a river, Lily saw a man sitting at the edge with tears in his eyes. She approached him and asked what was wrong.

The man told her that he had been holding onto anger and bitterness towards someone who had wronged him, and it was tearing him apart inside. He had come to the bridge to try and find some peace, but he couldn't seem to let go of his pain.

Lily listened to the man's story, and she realized that she was holding onto the same kind of pain. In that moment, she made a decision to let go of her grudge and forgive her friend. It wasn't easy, but she knew that it was the only way to find peace and freedom from her pain.

As Lily and the man talked, they realized that forgiveness was like a bridge that could help them cross over from pain to peace. It was a difficult journey, but it was one that was worth taking.

Over time, Lily found that she was able to let go of her anger and resentment. She began to see the good in her friend, and she realized that holding onto the past was only hurting her. She felt lighter and more free, and she knew that forgiveness was the key to her happiness.

The man, too, found peace through forgiveness. He was able to let go of his pain and move forward in his life with a new sense of freedom and joy.

As they parted ways, Lily and the man realized that the bridge of forgiveness was not just a physical bridge, but a bridge of the heart. It connected them to each other and to all those who had ever felt the pain of betrayal and hurt. It was a bridge of hope and healing, and they knew that it was one that they would cross again and again throughout their lives.

9

The River of Gratitude: Flowing with Thankfulness and Appreciation

O nce upon a time, there was a young woman named Maya who lived in a small village near a river. Maya had always been a hard-working and driven individual, constantly striving for success and achieving her goals. However, one day she realized that she had become so focused on her own accomplishments that she had forgotten to appreciate the blessings in her life.

Feeling lost and disconnected, Maya decided to take a walk along the river to clear her mind. As she walked, she noticed the beauty of the world around her - the vibrant colors of the flowers, the rustling of the leaves in the breeze, and the glistening of the water in the sunlight. She realized how much she had taken these things for granted in her pursuit of success.

Suddenly, she heard a soft voice behind her. "Do you see how much beauty there is in the world?" it said. She turned around to see an old woman with a kind smile on her face. "I do," Maya replied. "But I've been so focused on my own achievements that I've forgotten to appreciate it."

The old woman nodded knowingly. "It's easy to get lost in the pursuit of success," she said. "But it's important to remember that success is not just about personal achievements. It's also about the connections we make with others and the blessings we receive from the world around us."

Maya took the old woman's words to heart and decided to start a gratitude journal, writing down at least three things she was thankful for each day. At first, it was difficult to find things to be grateful for, but as time went on, Maya began to see the world in a new light. She noticed the small things that brought her joy - a kind word from a friend, a beautiful sunset, the taste of her favorite food.

As she became more grateful, Maya also became more connected to those around her. She began to see the beauty in each person she met, regardless of their flaws or differences. Her relationships with her family and friends grew stronger, and she felt more fulfilled than ever before.

Maya realized that gratitude had become like a river flowing through her life, bringing her peace, joy, and a sense of connectedness to the world around her. She knew that no matter what challenges came her way, she could always return to this river and find solace in the flow of thankfulness and appreciation.

From that day forward, Maya lived her life with a grateful heart, always appreciating the blessings in her life and sharing her gratitude with those around her.

10

The Path of Authenticity: Embracing Your True Self and Finding Freedom

I n a small village, there lived a young girl named Mei. She was a very introverted and reserved person, who always tried to blend in with the crowd to avoid being noticed. Mei had always struggled to express her true self, fearing judgment and rejection from others. She would often put on a façade to conform to societal norms and expectations, losing her authenticity in the process.

One day, while walking through the forest, Mei stumbled upon a wise old woman who was known to be a spiritual guide in the village. The old woman sensed Mei's discomfort and asked her what was troubling her. Mei explained her fears and struggles with authenticity, and how she felt trapped in her own skin.

The old woman smiled and told Mei a story about a caterpillar that had been living its entire life on a tree branch, afraid to leave its comfort zone. But one day, it felt a burning desire to transform into a butterfly and spread its wings. It knew that it had to leave the safety of the branch and venture into the unknown to fulfill its destiny. And so, it took a leap of faith and transformed into a beautiful butterfly, discovering a world of endless possibilities.

The old woman explained that just like the caterpillar, Mei needed to take a leap of faith and embrace her true self to fulfill her potential. She encouraged Mei to take small steps towards authenticity, like speaking her mind or pursuing her interests, and to trust in the process.

With the old woman's words of wisdom echoing in her mind, Mei began to slowly shed her old skin and embrace her true self. She started to speak her mind, pursue her passions, and stand up for what she believed in. Over time, Mei's confidence grew, and she found herself attracting genuine friendships and opportunities that aligned with her authentic self.

Mei realized that true freedom comes from within, and that being true to oneself is the key to living a fulfilling life. She continued to grow and transform, just like the caterpillar who had become a butterfly, spreading its wings and soaring to new heights.

11

The Garden of Resilience: Growing Stronger Through Adversity

I n a small village, there lived a farmer who was known for his beautiful garden. People from all around would come to admire the colorful flowers, towering trees, and luscious fruits that grew in his garden. However, not many knew about the struggles and challenges the farmer had to face to create and maintain his garden.

One year, a terrible storm hit the village, causing damage and destruction all around. The farmer's garden was not spared either. Trees were uprooted, flowers were crushed, and the fruits were scattered all around. The farmer was heartbroken to see his hard work being destroyed in a matter of hours. He sat in despair, wondering if he would ever be able to bring his garden back to life.

However, the farmer was a resilient man. He refused to let the storm break his spirit. He got up and started working on his garden again. Day after day, he toiled under the sun, planting new saplings, watering the soil, and nurturing the plants. His hands were rough, and his back ached, but he did not give up.

Months passed, and slowly but steadily, the garden started to come back to life. The flowers bloomed once again, the trees grew taller, and the fruits ripened on the branches. The farmer smiled as he watched the garden flourish once again.

People who came to visit the garden were amazed to see the beauty of the place. They asked the farmer how he managed to revive his garden after such a devastating storm. The farmer simply smiled and said, "It's the resilience of the plants that made this garden beautiful. I just had to provide them with the right conditions to grow."

The farmer's garden became a symbol of resilience for the people in the village. Whenever they faced adversity, they thought of the farmer and his garden and found the strength to carry on. The garden was not just a source of beauty and nourishment, but it also became a source of inspiration.

In life, we too face storms and challenges that can break us down. However, it is our resilience that helps us stand up and face the adversity head-on. Like the farmer's garden, we too can come back to life after a storm, but it requires patience, determination, and hard work. As the farmer said, it is the right conditions that help us grow, and we must strive to create those conditions for ourselves and others.

12

The Garden of Courage: Cultivating Bravery and Overcoming Fear

I n a beautiful garden, there lived a little sapling named Lily. Lily was a small plant and felt inadequate compared to the other big trees around her. She often felt that she would never grow as tall or as strong as them. One day, a storm hit the garden, and the winds were strong. The big trees were swaying and bending, but little Lily was being tossed around mercilessly.

The wind was blowing with such ferocity that Lily thought she would break. She tried to hold on to the ground with her small roots, but the wind was too strong. Just as she thought she would give up, she saw something that filled her with hope. The big trees around her were standing tall again, but they were all bent and crooked from the wind.

She realized that the big trees may look stronger, but they were not as flexible as she was. They were not able to bend and sway with the wind, which is what saved them from being uprooted. Lily learned that being small and flexible was not a weakness, but a strength.

From that day forward, Lily was no longer afraid of storms. She welcomed them, knowing that it was an opportunity for her to prove her resilience. She grew tall and strong, and although she was still small compared to the other trees, she was now proud of her size and what she had accomplished.

The other trees in the garden noticed Lily's growth and resilience, and they respected her for it. They realized that being strong was not just about being big, but about being able to withstand life's storms.

Years went by, and Lily had grown into a beautiful, strong tree. One day, a young sapling came to her, looking up at her with admiration. "How did you become so strong and brave?" the sapling asked.

Lily smiled and said, "I learned that being small and flexible is not a weakness, but a strength. You just have to believe in yourself and never give up. And when life's storms come, just bend and sway with them, and you will come out stronger on the other side."

The young sapling nodded, understanding the lesson. And with that, Lily knew that she had passed on the gift of courage and resilience to another, just as someone had once passed it on to her.

13

The Bridge of Resilience: Crossing Over to Strength and Endurance

O nce upon a time, there was a young man named Jack who lived in a small village near a river. One day, while walking along the river, Jack saw a bridge that had been destroyed due to a storm. He realized that the only way to cross the river was to swim, which was dangerous and difficult.

Jack was not a good swimmer, but he knew he had to get to the other side. He took a deep breath and plunged into the water. The current was strong, and Jack struggled to stay afloat. Just when he thought he couldn't make it, he saw a rope hanging from the broken bridge. He grabbed hold of it and slowly pulled himself towards the other side.

With great effort, Jack finally made it to the other side of the river. He was exhausted but relieved that he had made it safely. He realized that the rope was a symbol of resilience, something that helped him overcome his fear and difficulties.

From that day on, Jack began to develop a sense of resilience. He faced every challenge with determination and never gave up, even when things seemed impossible. He learned to be patient and to keep going, even when the going got tough.

Years passed, and Jack became a successful businessman. He always attributed his success to the lessons he learned on that fateful day at the river. He understood that life was full of obstacles and challenges, but he also knew that with resilience, he could overcome them all.

One day, while walking along the river, Jack saw that the bridge had been rebuilt. It was stronger and sturdier than before, and he realized that the villagers had come together to rebuild it, even after the storm had destroyed it. He understood that resilience was not just an individual trait, but something that could be shared and nurtured within a community.

From that day on, Jack became a mentor to the young people in the village, teaching them the value of resilience and the importance of coming together to face challenges. He encouraged them to never give up, even in the face of adversity, and to always remember that the bridge of resilience can be crossed by anyone who is willing to try.

In the end, Jack knew that the lessons he had learned about resilience had been the most valuable gift he had ever received. He knew that it was not just about crossing a river, but about crossing over to a life filled with strength, endurance, and the courage to face any challenge that came his way.

14

The Forest of Reflection: Finding Inner Clarity and Insight Through Self-Examination

In the heart of a dense forest, there was a small clearing where a wise old sage resided. He was known for his ability to help those who sought clarity and insight. Many people traveled from far and wide to seek his guidance.

One day, a young traveler stumbled upon the clearing and approached the sage. The young man was feeling lost and uncertain about his path in life. The sage invited him to sit down and asked him what was troubling him.

The young man explained that he had been traveling for many months, trying to find his purpose and passion in life. He felt like he was wandering aimlessly, without direction or clarity.

The sage listened intently and then asked the young man to

follow him into the forest. They walked in silence for a while until they reached a calm and serene pond. The water was still, and the reflection of the trees was crystal clear.

The sage instructed the young man to sit quietly by the pond and to focus on his reflection in the water. He told him to observe his thoughts as they came and went, without judgment or attachment.

The young man did as he was instructed, and after some time, he began to feel a sense of peace and clarity. As he looked at his reflection in the water, he realized that the answer to his question had been inside him all along. He had been searching for something outside himself when it had been inside him all along.

The sage then explained that the forest was a metaphor for our mind. Our thoughts are like the trees that grow in the forest, sometimes wild and tangled, and sometimes serene and still. By observing our thoughts without judgment or attachment, we can find clarity and insight into our true nature.

The young man thanked the sage and left the clearing feeling renewed and empowered. He realized that the answers he was seeking were within him all along, and that he just needed to quiet his mind to find them.

From that day on, the young man continued his journey with a newfound sense of purpose and direction. He understood that the forest of his mind would always have wild and tangled thoughts, but by observing them with awareness and acceptance, he could find inner peace and clarity.

15

The Circle of Empowerment: Supporting Others and Encouraging Positive Change

Once upon a time, there was a small village nestled in a lush forest. The villagers were kind and hardworking, but they often struggled to make ends meet. One day, a young girl named Maya decided to take matters into her own hands and start a community garden.

Maya went door to door, asking her neighbors if they would be interested in participating in the project. Many were skeptical at first, but Maya's enthusiasm and passion were contagious. Soon, a group of villagers came together to clear a patch of land and start planting vegetables.

At first, progress was slow, and many of the villagers doubted that the garden would ever amount to much. But Maya refused to give up. She encouraged everyone to keep working hard, even when the sun was hot and their backs were sore. Slowly but surely, the garden began to flourish.

As the garden grew, so did the sense of community among the villagers. They would gather to tend to the plants, share stories, and enjoy the fruits of their labor together. The garden had become a symbol of their resilience and determination in the face of adversity.

One day, a traveler passed through the village and was amazed by what he saw. He had never seen such a beautiful garden in such an unexpected place. He asked Maya how she had managed to create something so wonderful, and she simply smiled and said, "We did it together."

The traveler was moved by Maya's words and by the spirit of the village. He decided to make a donation to the garden, which allowed them to expand their efforts and provide fresh produce to even more people. Word of their success began to spread, and soon other villages began to follow their example.

Maya had shown the villagers that when they came together and worked towards a common goal, they could achieve great things. She had empowered them to take control of their own lives and make a positive change in their community. And in doing so, she had inspired others to do the same.

As the years went by, the garden continued to thrive, and Maya became a beloved leader in the village. She had shown everyone the power of working together, and had created a circle of empowerment that would continue to inspire others for generations to come.

16

The Ocean of Hope: Finding Optimism and Possibility in the Face of Adversity

In a small fishing village on the coast of Japan, there lived a young girl named Hana. Hana had grown up in a family of fishermen and had always been fascinated by the vast ocean that surrounded her home. She would often spend hours sitting on the rocky shore, watching the waves crash against the rocks and dreaming of what lay beyond the horizon.

One day, a massive storm struck the village, destroying boats and homes and leaving many families in despair. Hana's family was one of the hardest hit, losing their boat and all of their belongings. Hana felt overwhelmed by the sudden change and was unsure of how her family would recover.

But Hana refused to give up hope. She spent hours each day

helping her family rebuild their home and even went door to door in the village, asking for work so that she could earn money to help her family buy a new boat.

Despite the challenges, Hana's determination and positive attitude never wavered. She drew strength from the ocean, remembering its vastness and its ability to both create and destroy. Hana knew that if the ocean could endure storms and continue to bring new life to the shore, then she too could overcome the challenges she faced.

As the weeks went by, Hana's hard work paid off. She was able to save enough money to purchase a small boat for her family, and they slowly began to rebuild their lives. The village came together to support each other, and Hana's strength and resilience inspired others to stay hopeful and positive.

Years later, Hana had become a successful fisherman in her own right, and the memory of the storm had faded into the background. But whenever she faced new challenges, she would return to the ocean, finding comfort in its vastness and the hope it brought her.

Hana's story reminds us that even in the midst of adversity, hope and resilience can lead us to new possibilities. Like the ocean, we can weather storms and find the strength to rebuild and start anew.

17

The Path of Growth: Navigating Challenges and Embracing Opportunities for Personal Development

I n a small village nestled in the mountains, there lived a young woman named Mei. She was known for her gentle spirit and kind heart, but she often struggled with feelings of inadequacy and self-doubt. One day, Mei decided to take a walk in the forest to clear her mind and reflect on her life.

As she wandered along the winding paths, Mei stumbled upon a small sapling struggling to grow amidst the dense underbrush. She felt drawn to the tiny plant, and decided to take it under her care. She tended to the sapling, watering it daily and making sure it received plenty of sunlight.

Days turned into weeks, and weeks turned into months. As

Mei watched the sapling grow taller and stronger with each passing day, she began to realize the parallels between the tree's growth and her own journey of self-discovery. She saw how the sapling had started out small and fragile, much like how she had once felt. But with time and care, it had become resilient and unyielding.

Mei began to see herself in a new light, recognizing the strength and resilience she had built within herself over the years. She realized that her struggles and challenges had helped her grow and become the person she was today.

With a newfound sense of confidence and purpose, Mei decided to use her experience to help others in her village. She started volunteering at a local community center, offering her time and support to those in need. Through her actions, Mei inspired others to believe in themselves and see the strength within them.

As time passed, Mei's sapling grew into a towering tree, providing shade and shelter for all those who passed beneath it. Its strength and resilience were a reminder of Mei's own journey, and a symbol of the power of growth and transformation.

Through her experiences, Mei had discovered the path of growth. She had learned that life's challenges were opportunities for personal development, and that with time and care, even the smallest seed could grow into something powerful and strong. Mei had found her purpose, and was using her strength to help others find theirs.

18

The Dance of Authenticity: Expressing Your True Self and Embracing Individuality

O nce upon a time, there was a young girl named Ava who loved to dance. Ava had a passion for ballet, but she felt like she was always playing a role when she performed. She wanted to dance from her heart and express her true self. One day, Ava's dance teacher announced that the school would be performing a contemporary dance for the annual recital, and Ava saw this as an opportunity to break free from her constraints and express her authenticity.

During rehearsals, Ava struggled with the choreography. She found herself slipping back into her old habits of trying to be perfect and hiding her true self. Her dance teacher, noticing Ava's struggle, pulled her aside and said, "Ava, I can see you're holding back. Remember, dance is about expressing yourself, not about trying to be perfect. Let go of your fears and just dance from your heart."

Ava took her teacher's words to heart and decided to let go of her fears. She started to dance with freedom and joy, expressing herself in ways she never had before. As she danced, she felt a new sense of power and confidence within herself. She realized that when she danced from her true self, she was truly beautiful.

On the night of the recital, Ava took the stage with her fellow dancers. As they began to perform, Ava felt a new energy within her. She danced with power and grace, expressing her true self without any hesitation. The audience was captivated by her performance, and she received a standing ovation at the end of the dance.

After the show, Ava's dance teacher approached her and said, "Ava, I am so proud of you. You danced with authenticity and showed the world your true self. You are a beautiful dancer, but more importantly, you are a beautiful person."

From that day forward, Ava continued to dance with authenticity and to embrace her individuality. She learned that being true to herself was the key to her success, both on and off the stage. She went on to become a renowned contemporary dancer, inspiring others to express themselves and to embrace their true selves as well.

The story of Ava reminds us that authenticity is the foundation of true success and fulfillment. When we let go of our fears and embrace our true selves, we tap into our own unique power and potential. So let us all embrace our true selves and dance the dance of authenticity.

19

The Mountain of Perseverance: Climbing Higher Through Persistence and Determination

There was once a young man named Jack who dreamed of becoming a professional mountain climber. He had always been fascinated by the breathtaking views from the peaks of the world's highest mountains and wanted nothing more than to experience them firsthand.

One day, Jack decided to embark on his first solo climb up a nearby mountain. He set out early in the morning, full of excitement and anticipation. However, as he made his way up the steep incline, he encountered unexpected challenges that tested his endurance and determination.

First, he encountered a narrow ledge that required him to crawl on his hands and knees along a cliff face. His heart pounded in his chest as he struggled to maintain his balance, but he refused to give up.

Next, he encountered a sudden snowstorm that made it difficult to see more than a few feet in front of him. The biting cold seemed to seep into his bones, but he pressed on, determined to reach the summit.

Finally, after hours of strenuous climbing, Jack emerged at the top of the mountain. The breathtaking view of the surrounding landscape was more beautiful than he could have ever imagined, and he felt a sense of accomplishment wash over him.

Over the years, Jack continued to pursue his passion for mountain climbing. He faced many more challenges along the way, including broken bones, harsh weather conditions, and even the tragic loss of a fellow climber. But through it all, he remained steadfast in his commitment to his dream.

As he gained more experience and skill, Jack became known as one of the best mountain climbers in the world. He continued to push himself to new heights, always striving to reach the summit of even the most difficult mountains.

Through his perseverance and determination, Jack proved that anything is possible with hard work and dedication. He inspired countless others to pursue their own dreams, no matter how daunting they may seem.

And as he stood atop each new mountain, gazing out at the world below, he knew that the challenges he had faced along the way had only made him stronger and more resilient. For Jack, the mountain of perseverance had become a symbol of everything he had achieved and everything he had yet to accomplish.

20

The River of Graciousness: Flowing with Grace and Compassion Toward Yourself and Others

In a small village nestled in a valley, there lived a woman named Maya. She was known for her kindness and gentle nature. She had a heart of gold, and everyone in the village loved her. One day, Maya found out that she had been diagnosed with a rare and incurable disease. Her whole world turned upside down, and she felt like giving up.

Maya's family and friends rallied around her, trying to lift her spirits. But no matter how much they tried, she couldn't shake off the feeling of despair. One evening, as she sat alone by the river, feeling sorry for herself, she saw a small bird struggling in the water. Without hesitation, Maya jumped in and saved the bird.

As she cradled the bird in her hands, Maya realized that she had been so consumed by her own problems that she had forgotten to be grateful for the blessings in her life. She realized that she had been taking her health and the love of her family and friends for granted. She also realized that she needed to be more gracious and compassionate toward herself and others.

The next day, Maya decided to spend time volunteering at a local shelter for the homeless. She helped prepare meals, cleaned the shelter, and spent time listening to the stories of the people there. As she listened, Maya realized that everyone had their own struggles and that the world would be a better place if people showed more grace and compassion toward each other.

Maya's experience at the shelter changed her life. She began to look for ways to show more grace and compassion in her daily life. She started small by smiling at strangers, offering kind words to those who were struggling, and taking time to appreciate the little things in life.

As Maya's health declined, her spirit grew stronger. She realized that her life was not just about her, but about the impact she could have on others. She continued to spread love and kindness wherever she went, and her community was better for it.

When Maya passed away, the whole village mourned her loss. But they also celebrated the legacy she had left behind - a legacy of graciousness, compassion, and love. Maya's life had been a shining example of how one person can make a difference in the world, and her memory lived on in the hearts of those she had touched.

21

The Circle of Inspiration: Sparking Creativity and Passion Through Encouragement and Support

Once upon a time, there was a small village nestled at the base of a great mountain range. The villagers were hardworking and industrious, but they often felt stuck in their daily routines, lacking inspiration and creativity.

One day, a young traveler arrived in the village, carrying with her a small box of seeds. She went from house to house, offering the seeds to the villagers and encouraging them to plant them in their gardens. Many of the villagers were hesitant, as they had never seen such unusual seeds before, but a few brave souls decided to take a chance.

The traveler left the village, but over the following weeks, the seeds began to sprout and grow. The villagers were astonished to see such beautiful and unique plants growing in their gardens. They began to talk to one another, sharing stories about the different plants they were growing and how they were caring for them.

As the plants grew taller and stronger, the villagers began to feel a renewed sense of energy and inspiration. They started to experiment with new recipes using the fruits and vegetables from their gardens, and some even began to create artwork inspired by the colors and shapes of the plants.

One day, the traveler returned to the village and was amazed to see the transformation that had taken place. The villagers were full of energy and creativity, and their gardens were bursting with life. The traveler smiled, knowing that the seeds she had brought had been the catalyst for this amazing change.

The villagers gathered around the traveler, thanking her for bringing the seeds that had transformed their lives. They asked her how they could repay her, but the traveler simply smiled and said, "You have already repaid me by cultivating these beautiful gardens and inspiring one another. Keep sharing your creativity and supporting one another, and your village will continue to thrive."

The traveler stayed with the villagers for a few more days, sharing stories and ideas with them. When it was time for her to leave, the villagers thanked her again and promised to continue to nurture their gardens and inspire one another.

Years went by, and the village became known throughout the land for its beautiful gardens and creative inhabitants. People from far and wide came to visit and learn from the villagers, and they all marveled at the beauty and inspiration that had grown from such small seeds.

And so, the Circle of Inspiration continued to grow and spread, fueled by the energy and passion of those who nurtured it.

22

The Path of Resilient Love: Overcoming Obstacles and Nurturing Relationships

There was a couple named Maya and Jacob who had been together for over 20 years. They had gone through many ups and downs in their relationship but had always managed to come out stronger on the other side. However, one day, Jacob received news that he had been diagnosed with a serious illness.

Maya was devastated but knew that she had to be strong for both of them. She took on the role of caregiver, making sure Jacob was taking his medications and going to his appointments. Despite the challenges they faced, their love for each other only grew stronger.

As the days turned into weeks and the weeks turned into months, Maya found herself becoming exhausted and overwhelmed. She began to feel like she wasn't doing enough and started to doubt herself. One day, while sitting in the waiting room at the hospital, Maya met another woman who was going through a similar experience with her husband. They struck up a conversation and Maya found herself feeling a sense of relief knowing that she wasn't alone.

Over time, Maya became part of a support group for caregivers of loved ones with illnesses. She found comfort in being able to share her experiences with others who understood what she was going through. With the help of her support group, Maya was able to find the strength to continue caring for Jacob with renewed energy and compassion.

As Jacob's health began to improve, Maya realized that their relationship had grown even stronger through this difficult time. They had learned to lean on each other and to appreciate the moments they had together. Maya knew that their love was resilient and could withstand any challenge that came their way.

Years later, Jacob's health had fully recovered and they looked back on that time in their lives with gratitude for the love and support they had shared. Maya realized that their journey had taught her the power of resilience and the importance of seeking support from others. She had learned that love can overcome even the most difficult of obstacles and that through it all, she had become a stronger and more resilient person.

23

The Forest of Renewal: Rejuvenating Your Spirit and Embracing Change

Once there was a traveler who found herself lost in a dense forest. She had been walking for hours, but the more she walked, the more lost she became. She was exhausted, hungry, and thirsty, and she feared that she would never find her way out.

As the sun began to set, the traveler came upon a clearing in the forest. In the center of the clearing stood a tall tree, its branches reaching up toward the sky. The traveler approached the tree and noticed that it was covered in small buds. She realized that this tree was a symbol of hope and renewal, and she decided to make camp beneath its branches.

Over the next few days, the traveler rested and ate the fruits that had fallen from the tree. As she rested, she began to reflect on her life and the direction it was taking. She realized that she had been living on autopilot, going through the motions of life without ever really stopping to consider what she truly wanted.

The traveler knew that she needed to make a change. She decided to use her time in the forest as an opportunity for renewal and introspection. She explored the forest, taking in the beauty of the trees and the wildlife. She allowed herself to be fully present in each moment, without worrying about the past or the future.

As the days passed, the traveler noticed that the buds on the tree had begun to bloom. The tree was now covered in beautiful flowers of all colors, each one a symbol of renewal and growth. The traveler realized that just as the tree had undergone a transformation, so too had she.

When the time came to leave the forest, the traveler felt a sense of gratitude and contentment. She knew that the forest had given her the space and time she needed to renew her spirit and embrace change. As she stepped out of the forest and back onto the path of her life, she felt ready to face whatever challenges lay ahead.

The traveler carried the lessons of the forest with her always, remembering the power of renewal and the importance of taking time for introspection. Whenever she faced a difficult situation, she thought back to the tree in the clearing and the beauty of its blooming buds. She knew that just as the tree had bloomed again, she too could find renewal and growth in the face of any challenge.

24

The Ocean of Forgiveness: Letting Go of Grudges and Finding Peace

Once upon a time, there was an old man who lived by the ocean. He had a deep-rooted grudge against a person from his past, and it weighed heavily on his heart. Every day, he would walk along the shore and stare out into the endless sea, feeling bitterness and resentment.

One day, a young girl approached him and asked why he always looked so sad. The old man explained his long-standing grudge and how it had consumed his life. The girl listened patiently, and then she said, "Have you ever considered forgiving this person?"

The old man was taken aback. He had never thought about forgiveness before, and the idea seemed impossible. But the girl continued, "Forgiveness is like the ocean. It's vast and deep, and it has the power to wash away all your pain and hurt. Just like the ocean, forgiveness can bring you peace and freedom."

The old man thought about what the girl had said and decided to give forgiveness a chance. He started by writing a letter to the person he had been holding a grudge against, expressing his hurt and anger but also his willingness to forgive. When he finished writing, he went to the ocean and tossed the letter into the waves, symbolically letting go of his resentment.

As the days passed, the old man began to feel lighter and happier. He no longer felt burdened by his grudge and found that he could enjoy life once again. He started to see the beauty of the ocean and the world around him, and he even began to make new friends.

One day, the old man saw the young girl again and thanked her for helping him find peace through forgiveness. She smiled and said, "Remember, the ocean of forgiveness is always here for you, and so am I."

From that day forward, the old man made it a habit to walk along the shore every day, not to dwell on his past but to appreciate the beauty of the present and the possibilities of the future. He had learned that forgiveness was not only for the person he forgave but also for himself, and it had opened up a whole new world of joy and gratitude.

The ocean continued to remind him of the power of forgiveness, and whenever he looked out into its vast expanse, he was reminded of the endless possibilities of forgiveness and the peace it could bring.

25

The Mountain of Transformation: Reimagining Your Life Through Growth and Change

In a small village nestled in the mountains, there lived a young woman named Mei who dreamed of leaving her quiet life behind and traveling the world. She was eager to experience new cultures and ways of life, but her family was against the idea, fearing for her safety and wellbeing. Mei was torn between her desire to explore and the expectations placed upon her by her loved ones.

One day, Mei decided to climb the highest peak in the mountain range, hoping that the challenge would help her find clarity and guidance. She packed a small bag of supplies and set off early in the morning. As she made her way up the steep trail, she encountered many obstacles, including rocky terrain and harsh weather conditions. But she persevered, taking each step with determination and focus.

After several hours of climbing, Mei reached the summit of the mountain. She was greeted by a breathtaking view of the world below, and a sense of awe and wonder filled her heart. As she sat down to rest, she realized that the journey had taught her a valuable lesson.

Just like the mountain, Mei had gone through many changes and challenges in her life. But instead of letting them defeat her, she had used them to grow and transform. She had developed resilience and strength, and now, she was ready to face whatever the world had in store for her.

With a renewed sense of purpose, Mei descended the mountain, eager to start her new life. She knew that it wouldn't be easy, but she was confident in her abilities and excited to see where her path would lead her.

Years later, Mei returned to her village, having traveled the world and gained a wealth of experiences and knowledge. Her family was amazed at the confident and self-assured woman she had become, and they welcomed her back with open arms.

Mei realized that her journey had not only transformed her own life but had also inspired others to pursue their dreams and overcome their own challenges. She knew that the mountain had been a powerful symbol of transformation, reminding her that growth and change were always possible, no matter how difficult the journey may be.

26

The Circle of Gratitude: Fostering a Heart of Thankfulness and Joy

I n a small village nestled in the heart of the mountains, there was a young girl named Mei. Mei lived with her parents and two younger brothers in a modest house on the outskirts of the village. Despite their simple life, Mei's parents instilled in their children the importance of gratitude and kindness.

One day, Mei's village was hit by a massive storm, and many homes were destroyed. Mei and her family were fortunate enough to have a sturdy house, but they knew that their neighbors were not as lucky. Mei's parents decided to open their home to those who needed shelter, and soon, their house was filled with people seeking refuge from the storm.

As Mei watched her parents and siblings share their home and resources with their neighbors, she couldn't help but feel overwhelmed with gratitude. She realized that they had so much to be thankful for, even in the midst of a disaster. Mei began to look for small things to be grateful for each day, like a warm meal or a comfortable bed to sleep in.

As she practiced gratitude, Mei's heart became lighter, and she began to see the world around her with new eyes. She noticed the beauty of the mountains that surrounded her village and the kindness of her friends and family. Mei even found joy in the midst of difficult situations, knowing that there was always something to be grateful for.

Years passed, and Mei grew up to be a kind and compassionate woman, always willing to lend a helping hand to those in need. Her parents often told her that her grateful heart was what inspired them to be better people. Mei knew that her gratitude had not only changed her life, but the lives of those around her.

One day, Mei's village was hit by another storm, but this time, Mei was ready. She and her family opened their home once again to those who needed shelter, and Mei shared her gratitude with everyone she met. As they sat huddled together, safe from the storm outside, Mei's neighbors thanked her and her family for their generosity.

Mei simply smiled and replied, "I have so much to be grateful for, and I want to share that gratitude with others. It's what makes life so beautiful." And as Mei looked around at the faces of those around her, she knew that her circle of gratitude had grown a little larger, and that was something to be truly thankful for.

27

The Bridge of Acceptance: Embracing Yourself and Others with Unconditional Love

Once upon a time, there was a young woman named Lily who struggled with acceptance. She was always worried about what others thought of her and constantly sought their approval. This need for validation caused her to change who she was and hide her true self.

One day, Lily went on a walk in the park and stumbled upon a beautiful bridge. As she walked across it, she noticed something peculiar. Each plank of wood had a message engraved on it, and as she read them, she felt a sense of peace wash over her.

The first plank read, "Acceptance begins with self-love." Lily realized that she had been seeking acceptance from others without truly accepting herself. She decided to start loving and accepting herself for who she was.

The second plank read, "Everyone has their own journey, accept them for where they are." Lily realized that everyone was on their own unique path, and it was not her place to judge them or try to change them.

The third plank read, "Acceptance does not mean agreement, but it does mean respect." Lily learned that she could disagree with someone's beliefs or actions but still treat them with kindness and respect.

The fourth plank read, "Acceptance brings peace." Lily realized that when she accepted herself and others, she felt a sense of calm and tranquility.

As Lily walked across the bridge, she felt a weight lifting off her shoulders. She realized that true acceptance was not about changing who she was to fit in or seeking validation from others, but about loving and respecting herself and others for who they were.

From that day forward, Lily started practicing acceptance in her daily life. She stopped trying to please others and instead focused on being true to herself. She also started accepting others for who they were, no matter their differences.

Lily realized that the bridge was not just a physical structure, but a metaphor for her journey towards acceptance. She continued to cross it every day, reading the engraved planks and reminding herself of the lessons she had learned.

Thanks to the bridge of acceptance, Lily found peace and happiness in being true to herself and accepting others for who they were. She learned that acceptance was not only a gift to others but also to herself.

28

The Dance of Liberation: Breaking Free from Limitations and Embracing Freedom

Once upon a time, in a small village in a distant land, there was a young woman named Maya. She lived a life that was comfortable but unfulfilling. Maya had dreams and aspirations, but she was afraid to take the leap and pursue them. She felt trapped by the expectations of her family and society, and her fear of failure kept her from stepping out of her comfort zone.

One day, Maya was walking in the forest when she stumbled upon a group of birds. They were singing and dancing with such joy and freedom that Maya couldn't help but be mesmerized. She watched them for a while, envious of their carefree spirits and their ability to express themselves without fear or inhibition.

As she continued her walk, Maya realized that she wanted to experience that same sense of freedom and liberation. She wanted to break free from her limitations and embrace a life of joy and possibility. With that thought, she started to dance.

At first, Maya was hesitant, unsure of what others might think of her. But the more she danced, the more she felt a sense of release and liberation. She moved her body with abandon, feeling the wind on her face and the sun on her skin. In that moment, she felt truly alive.

As Maya continued to dance, she realized that her fears and insecurities had been holding her back. She had been living a life that was not true to herself, trying to fit into a mold that was not meant for her. But now, she felt free to be who she was meant to be.

With that newfound sense of liberation, Maya decided to pursue her dreams. She started her own business, which had always been her passion, and poured her heart and soul into it. She faced many challenges and obstacles along the way, but she persevered with the same spirit of liberation and freedom that she had felt in the forest.

In the end, Maya's business was a great success, and she found a sense of fulfillment and joy that she had never known before. She continued to dance, not just physically, but in the way she lived her life - with a sense of freedom, liberation, and authenticity.

Maya's story is a reminder that we all have the power to break free from our limitations and embrace a life of liberation and joy. We just have to be willing to take that first step, to dance with abandon and let ourselves be who we truly are.

29

The Garden of Mindfulness: Cultivating Peace and Clarity Through Present Moment Awareness

Once there was a woman named Ava who was always busy and constantly on-the-go. She had a demanding job and a full social calendar, leaving her little time for herself. She found herself constantly feeling overwhelmed and stressed, with her mind racing a million miles a minute.

One day, a friend recommended that Ava try practicing mindfulness as a way to find more peace and clarity in her life. At first, Ava was skeptical - how could simply being present in the moment help her with her busy schedule? But after some research, she decided to give it a try.

Ava started small, setting aside just five minutes each day to sit in quiet and focus on her breath. At first, her mind would wander and she found it hard to sit still, but as she continued to practice, she found that her mind began to quiet down and she was able to be more present in the moment.

As Ava continued to practice mindfulness, she began to notice changes in her daily life. She found that she was able to focus more easily at work, and was able to manage her time better. She also found that she was more patient with her friends and family, and was able to truly be present with them when they spent time together.

One day, Ava decided to take a walk in a nearby garden to practice her mindfulness. As she strolled through the winding paths, she took in the beauty of the nature around her. She noticed the different colors of the flowers and the sound of the birds chirping. As she continued to walk, Ava felt a sense of calm and peace wash over her. She realized that mindfulness wasn't just about sitting in quiet, but could be practiced in everyday activities.

From that day forward, Ava continued to practice mindfulness and found that it brought her more peace, clarity, and joy in her life. She began to see the world in a different way, noticing small details that she had never paid attention to before. She also found that her relationships improved, as she was more present with her loved ones and able to truly connect with them.

Ava realized that mindfulness was not just a practice, but a way of life. By being present in the moment and practicing gratitude for the world around her, she found that life became more beautiful and fulfilling.

30

The Path of Courageous Vulnerability: Embracing Authenticity and Connection Through Openness

Sophie had always been a private person. She had been taught from a young age that vulnerability was a weakness, and that it was best to keep her emotions to herself. As a result, she had built up walls around herself, walls that kept others out and prevented her from truly connecting with anyone. But as she grew older, she began to feel a sense of loneliness, a feeling that there was something missing from her life.

One day, Sophie stumbled upon a quote that read, "Vulnerability is the birthplace of connection and the path to the feeling of worthiness. If it doesn't feel vulnerable, the sharing is probably not constructive." Those words struck a chord with her, and she realized that she had been missing out on something essential in life: the ability to connect with others on a deeper level.

Determined to break down her walls, Sophie began to practice vulnerability in small ways. She started by sharing her thoughts and feelings with close friends and family, even when it was uncomfortable. As she did so, she found that people responded positively, offering their own support and vulnerability in return.

One day, Sophie was invited to speak at a conference about her work in the tech industry. She was nervous, but determined to be open and honest about her experiences. As she took the stage, she felt her heart pounding in her chest. But as she began to speak, she found herself feeling more and more at ease. She shared her struggles, her successes, and her hopes for the future. When she finished, she was met with thunderous applause.

After the conference, Sophie received countless messages from people who had been inspired by her talk. They told her that her vulnerability had given them the courage to be more open in their own lives. And Sophie realized that by sharing her own story, she had given others permission to do the same.

From that day forward, Sophie continued to practice vulnerability in all areas of her life. She allowed herself to be seen, flaws and all, and found that she was met with love and acceptance. She realized that vulnerability wasn't a weakness, but rather a strength. By being open and honest with herself and others, she had found a sense of connection and meaning that she had been missing for so long.

Sophie's journey had taught her that it takes courage to be vulnerable, but the rewards are immeasurable. By embracing her true self and allowing others to see her for who she was, she had found a sense of liberation that she had never known was possible.

31

The River of Harmony: Finding Balance and Unity Amidst Diversity and Differences

Once upon a time, in a small village, there lived a diverse community of people who often found themselves at odds with one another. They had different beliefs, customs, and ways of life, which made it difficult for them to coexist peacefully. But deep down, they all yearned for harmony and unity.

One day, a wise elder decided to take action. He invited all the villagers to gather by the river that flowed through their community. There, he asked each person to bring a stone and place it in the river, creating a cairn that would grow taller and stronger as each person added their stone.

The villagers hesitated at first, unsure of what good it would do. But the elder urged them on, promising that it would help them find harmony and unity.

As the villagers placed their stones in the river, they started to notice something magical happening. The water flowed around the stones, creating a beautiful melody that sounded like a song. They watched as the river, stones, and the people all became one, moving together in perfect harmony.

The elder explained that just as the river flows around the stones, so too can they flow around their differences and find unity. He urged them to remember that each person's unique stone was important and necessary to create the beautiful harmony they witnessed.

The villagers left the river feeling inspired and grateful for the experience. They started to see each other in a different light, with a newfound respect for their differences. Over time, they learned to work together and found that they were able to accomplish great things.

The cairn in the river continued to grow, and whenever a new villager joined their community, they were invited to add their stone to the cairn. The river of harmony became a symbol of their unity and a reminder of the power of coming together.

From that day forward, whenever the villagers faced conflicts or challenges, they would gather by the river and remember the lesson of the cairn. They learned that by respecting each other's differences and finding harmony, they could achieve anything they set their minds to.

The river of harmony became a source of inspiration for generations to come, reminding them of the importance of finding balance and unity amidst diversity and differences.

32

The Garden of Resilient Joy: Cultivating Happiness and Contentment Through Adversity

In the midst of a bustling city, there was a small garden tended by a kind old man named Mr. Lee. Despite the constant noise and pollution, Mr. Lee's garden was a haven of peace and beauty. It was a place where people could come to relax, meditate, and connect with nature.

One day, a woman named Sarah stumbled upon Mr. Lee's garden. She had been feeling lost and hopeless ever since she lost her job and her relationship ended. She sat down on one of the benches and gazed at the flowers, trees, and pond. Despite the chaos of the city outside, she felt a sense of calm wash over her.

Mr. Lee approached her and asked her how she was doing. Sarah hesitated at first, but something about Mr. Lee's gentle and compassionate demeanor made her feel safe enough to open up to him. She shared her struggles with him, and he listened with a kind and understanding ear.

Mr. Lee shared with her his own story of resilience. He told her how he had survived the Japanese occupation of his hometown during World War II, and how he had lost everything he owned during the Korean War. He also told her how he had found solace and purpose in gardening, and how it had helped him to find joy even in the darkest of times.

Sarah was inspired by Mr. Lee's story. She realized that just like the plants in the garden, she too could find a way to bloom even in adversity. With Mr. Lee's guidance, she started to volunteer in the garden, learning about different plants and techniques for cultivation. She found that working in the garden gave her a sense of purpose and accomplishment, and she started to feel more hopeful about her future.

Over time, Sarah's relationship with Mr. Lee deepened. He became a mentor and a friend, offering her wisdom and guidance whenever she needed it. Through his teachings, Sarah learned how to cultivate a resilient and joyful spirit, even in the face of life's challenges.

Years later, when Mr. Lee passed away, Sarah inherited his garden. She continued to tend to it with the same love and care that he had, and she also passed on his teachings to others. The garden became a symbol of resilience and hope, a place where people could come to find peace and inspiration, just like Sarah had.

33

The Path of Radical Acceptance: Embracing Imperfection and Finding Inner Peace

Once upon a time, there was a young woman named Maya. Maya was an ambitious and driven individual, always striving for perfection in everything she did. She worked hard, went to the best schools, and had an impressive career, but she was always left feeling unsatisfied and incomplete.

One day, Maya came across a book on radical acceptance. The book talked about accepting oneself as they are, imperfections and all. Maya was skeptical at first, but she decided to give it a try. She started with small things, like accepting that she wasn't the best at cooking or that she had a tendency to procrastinate. As she practiced acceptance, she began to feel a sense of peace that she had never experienced before.

One day, Maya's boss assigned her a project that she was unfamiliar with. Maya was nervous and anxious about the task, fearing that she would fail and disappoint her boss. But instead of giving in to her fear, Maya decided to approach the project with radical acceptance. She accepted that she might make mistakes along the way, but that was okay because she was still learning and growing.

As Maya worked on the project, she realized that she was enjoying it more than she had anticipated. She was able to think creatively and outside of the box because she wasn't limiting herself to the idea of perfection. Maya was surprised to find that the project turned out to be a success and her boss was impressed with her work.

From that day on, Maya began to practice radical acceptance in all aspects of her life. She stopped judging herself for her mistakes and shortcomings and instead embraced them as opportunities for growth and learning. Maya learned that radical acceptance wasn't about giving up on self-improvement, but rather accepting and loving herself for who she was, imperfections and all.

Maya began to radiate a newfound sense of peace and inner strength that inspired those around her. Her friends and family noticed a positive change in her, and even strangers were drawn to her infectious energy.

Maya realized that true happiness and inner peace could only come from within and that it was up to her to create that for herself. From then on, Maya lived a life of radical acceptance, filled with love and compassion for herself and those around her.

34

The Circle of Authentic Connection: Building Meaningful Relationships Through Vulnerability

Once upon a time, in a small village nestled between two mountains, lived a woman named Maya. Maya was kind and generous, but she struggled with deep-seated insecurities that often left her feeling isolated and disconnected from others.

One day, Maya decided to attend a gathering at the village square. As she approached, she could hear the sound of laughter and conversation. Maya hesitated, feeling the familiar pang of anxiety. But she took a deep breath and reminded herself of her intention to connect with others.

As she entered the circle, Maya was greeted warmly by her neighbors. She sat down and listened as others shared stories and insights from their lives. Maya was surprised by the depth of honesty and vulnerability in the group. For the first time in a long time, she felt seen and heard.

Maya started attending the gatherings regularly, sharing her own experiences and listening to others with compassion and curiosity. She began to notice a shift within herself, as she allowed herself to be vulnerable and authentic in the presence of others.

Over time, Maya formed close bonds with several members of the circle. They shared their joys and sorrows, celebrated their successes, and supported each other through difficult times. Maya felt a sense of belonging that she had never experienced before.

One day, Maya's friend Raj approached her with a request. He wanted to start a new circle, focused specifically on building authentic connections and fostering vulnerability. He asked Maya to co-facilitate with him.

At first, Maya was hesitant. She didn't feel qualified to lead such a group. But Raj encouraged her, reminding her of the wisdom and insight she had gained through her own journey of vulnerability and connection.

Maya agreed, and together, she and Raj formed a new circle. They were amazed by the response - people came from all over the village to join them. Each week, they shared stories, laughter, tears, and moments of deep connection.

Maya felt grateful for the opportunity to give back to her

community in this way. She realized that her own struggles with vulnerability had opened a door to something beautiful - a network of authentic, caring relationships that brought her joy and purpose.

As the circle grew, Maya felt a renewed sense of confidence and belonging. She knew that she had found her place in the world - not just as an individual, but as a member of a supportive and loving community.

35

The Ocean of Compassionate Action: Making a Positive Difference in the World Through Kindness and Empathy

I n a small fishing village by the coast, there was a young girl named Maya who had a heart full of compassion. She would often visit the shore and watch the fishermen bring in their catch, but what caught her attention the most was the number of tiny fish that were caught in their nets. They were too small to be sold, and the fishermen would simply throw them back into the sea.

One day, Maya decided to collect all the tiny fish in a bucket and take them home with her. She spent the entire day taking care of them and nurturing them. She provided them with clean water, food, and a safe environment to grow. She even named each of the tiny fish and talked to them every day.

As time passed, the tiny fish began to grow bigger and stronger. Maya knew that they couldn't stay in the bucket forever, so she decided to release them back into the ocean. She went to the shore and gently poured the fish back into the water. As she watched them swim away, Maya felt a sense of joy and contentment that she had never felt before.

Maya's act of kindness didn't go unnoticed. The villagers soon learned about what she had done, and they were amazed by her compassion and empathy towards the tiny fish. They were inspired by her actions and began to think of ways they could also make a positive difference in the world.

Slowly but surely, the village began to transform. People started to take care of their environment, and they became more aware of the impact their actions had on the ocean and its inhabitants. They started to think about the future generations and the legacy they wanted to leave behind.

Maya's small act of compassion had created a ripple effect that spread throughout the village and beyond. Her kindness had inspired others to take action and make a positive difference in the world. Maya realized that even the smallest of actions can create a significant impact, and that everyone has the power to make a difference.

From that day forward, Maya became known as the "Compassionate Fishkeeper," and her story inspired people all over the world to make a positive difference in their own communities. She showed them that through acts of kindness, empathy, and compassion, they could make the world a better place for everyone, including the tiny fish in the sea.

36

The Bridge of Self-Compassion: Learning to Treat Yourself with Kindness and Forgiveness

Once upon a time, there was a woman named Lily who was very hard on herself. She always set high standards and goals for herself, and whenever she fell short of her expectations, she would beat herself up over it. Lily's self-talk was full of criticism and self-judgment, and she often felt like she was her own worst enemy.

One day, while taking a walk in the park, Lily noticed a beautiful bridge that she had never seen before. The bridge looked like it led to a peaceful garden on the other side of a small stream. As she approached the bridge, she saw a sign that read, "The Bridge of Self-Compassion."

Lily was curious and decided to cross the bridge. As she stepped onto it, she felt a sense of calm and tranquility wash over her. The sound of the flowing water below and the sight of the trees and flowers in the garden ahead made her feel at ease.

As she walked along the bridge, she noticed that there were affirmations and quotes written on the railings. One of them caught her eye: "Be kind to yourself, for you are the only companion you will have for the rest of your life."

Lily realized that she had been so focused on achieving her goals and being perfect that she had forgotten to be kind to herself. She took a deep breath and made a promise to herself to practice self-compassion from that moment on.

When she reached the other side of the bridge, she saw a small statue of a woman with her arms wrapped around herself in a loving embrace. The plaque at the base of the statue read, "Self-Compassion: The act of treating yourself with the same kindness, concern, and support that you would offer to a good friend."

Lily realized that she had been neglecting herself in ways that she would never have treated a friend. She made a vow to start treating herself with the same compassion and care that she would offer to someone she loved.

From that day on, Lily's self-talk changed. She started using kind and encouraging words instead of critical and judgmental ones. She allowed herself to make mistakes and learn from them instead of beating herself up over them.

The Bridge of Self-Compassion had taught her a valuable lesson: that being kind to oneself is an act of courage and strength, not weakness. She had crossed the bridge and found a new sense of self-love and acceptance on the other side.

37

The Mountain of Self-Discovery: Finding Your True Self Through Exploration and Reflection

Deep in the mountains, there was a small village where people lived a simple life. The villagers were content with their lives, but there was one person who yearned for something more. His name was Kian, and he often found himself gazing up at the mountains, wondering what lay beyond.

One day, Kian decided to embark on a journey of self-discovery. He packed some food and water and set out into the mountains. The climb was steep, and the air thin, but Kian was determined to reach the top.

As he climbed higher, Kian began to notice the subtle changes around him. The air grew cooler, the sky brighter, and the trees gave way to vast open spaces. He felt a sense of liberation and exhilaration as he gazed out at the stunning vista before him.

But the climb was not without its challenges. Kian encountered steep cliffs, treacherous ledges, and raging rivers. He had to use all his strength, skill, and determination to overcome each obstacle.

As Kian climbed higher and higher, he began to realize that the journey wasn't just about reaching the summit. It was about discovering himself, facing his fears, and pushing himself beyond his limits.

At last, after days of climbing, Kian reached the top of the mountain. He was awestruck by the sheer beauty of the landscape around him. He felt a deep sense of peace and clarity wash over him, as if he had finally found what he had been searching for all along.

Kian sat there, taking in the view, and realized that he had changed in profound ways. He had discovered his inner strength, resilience, and determination. He had faced his fears and learned to overcome them. And he had found a new sense of purpose and meaning in his life.

As Kian began his descent down the mountain, he knew that the journey of self-discovery was ongoing. But he also knew that he had the courage and resilience to face whatever challenges lay ahead. He had discovered that the path to self-discovery was not just about reaching the summit, but about the journey itself, and the person he had become along the way.

38

The Forest of Creative Healing: Using Art and Imagination to Overcome Trauma and Pain

Once upon a time, there was a woman named Sophia who had been through a lot of emotional trauma in her life. She had lost her parents at a young age, and had experienced several abusive relationships. Over time, she found it difficult to trust anyone and had become withdrawn and isolated.

One day, while walking through the forest, she stumbled upon a clearing where a group of artists were creating beautiful works of art. They invited her to join them, and she discovered that the act of creating was a healing process for her.

As she worked on her art, she found that it was a way to express her emotions in a safe and constructive way. She began to paint the pain and the hurt, and as she did, she felt a sense of release. She also found that she was able to tap into a part of herself that had been hidden away for a long time.

Through her art, Sophia was able to discover her own inner strength and resilience. She realized that she had the power to overcome her past and create a new future for herself.

Over time, Sophia became a regular at the forest art studio. She also began to share her work with others and found that her art was inspiring and healing for those who saw it. She started to teach art classes for people who had experienced trauma, and found that helping others was also a way to heal herself.

Through her art, Sophia was able to create a new life for herself. She found love, and was able to trust again. She also discovered that there was a great deal of beauty and joy in the world, and that she could be a part of it.

In the end, Sophia learned that healing is a process that requires patience and persistence. She also learned that the journey is worth it, and that there is a light at the end of the tunnel. Most importantly, she discovered that art was a powerful tool for healing and transformation, and that anyone can use it to overcome their own pain and trauma.

39

The Circle of Gracious Accountability: Taking Responsibility for Your Actions and Learning from Mistakes

I n a small village lived a young man named Ravi who was known for his laziness and carelessness. He had a habit of procrastinating everything and often missed his deadlines. He would come up with excuses for not completing his tasks on time and blame others for his mistakes. This attitude of his had made him unpopular among the villagers.

One day, the village elder organized a meeting of all the villagers to discuss the issue of Ravi's behavior. Everyone in the meeting agreed that Ravi needed to change his ways and become more accountable for his actions. The village elder suggested that they form a circle of gracious accountability where they would support Ravi in taking responsibility for his actions and encourage him to learn from his mistakes.

The circle of gracious accountability was formed, and Ravi was invited to join. He was hesitant at first but agreed to participate. In the circle, everyone shared their own experiences of taking responsibility for their actions and the positive outcomes that followed. They also listened to Ravi's side of the story and empathized with him. They encouraged him to take small steps towards becoming more accountable and celebrated his efforts along the way.

Over time, Ravi started to take his responsibilities more seriously. He began to meet his deadlines, completed his work on time, and apologized whenever he made mistakes. The villagers noticed the change in his behavior and appreciated his efforts. They also provided constructive feedback to help him improve further.

One day, Ravi's hard work paid off when he was given a task to organize a festival for the village. He took charge of the task and completed it successfully, making sure everything was done on time and with great care. The villagers were impressed with his efforts and thanked him for his work.

Ravi had learned the value of accountability and realized that taking responsibility for his actions not only benefited him but also those around him. He continued to participate in the circle of gracious accountability, and over time, he became a respected member of the village. The circle had taught him to be more accountable, and it had also helped him build meaningful relationships with the people in his community.

From that day on, Ravi made it his mission to spread the

message of gracious accountability to others. He shared his story with those who struggled with taking responsibility for their actions and encouraged them to join the circle. With the support of the villagers, Ravi had transformed from a careless and lazy young man to a responsible and respected member of the community.

40

The River of Mindful Communication: Building Stronger Connections Through Active Listening and Empathy

Once upon a time, there was a peaceful river that flowed through a bustling town. It was known as the River of Mindful Communication because it had the power to bring people together through the art of listening and empathy.

One day, a young man named Alex decided to take a walk by the river. As he strolled along the bank, he noticed a group of people gathered around a woman who was visibly upset. Alex walked closer and heard the woman expressing her frustration with a co-worker who wasn't understanding her point of view.

The group was quick to offer their opinions and advice, but Alex noticed that nobody was truly listening to the woman's feelings. So he stepped forward and asked if he could speak with her privately. She agreed, and Alex listened intently as she shared her thoughts and emotions.

He asked open-ended questions and made sure to reflect back what she was saying to show that he understood her perspective. Slowly but surely, the woman began to calm down and feel heard.

Together, they came up with a plan to approach her co-worker with a more empathetic and understanding attitude. And just like that, the woman walked away from the river feeling lighter and more hopeful.

As Alex continued his walk, he realized that the River of Mindful Communication was more than just a body of water - it was a way of life. He made a commitment to himself to practice active listening and empathy in all of his relationships, whether it be with his family, friends, or colleagues.

Over time, Alex became known as a trusted confidant and wise counselor. He helped many people navigate difficult situations by simply taking the time to listen and understand.

And as more and more people in the town began to adopt this way of communicating, the River of Mindful Communication flowed stronger than ever before. It brought people together, healed old wounds, and created a sense of unity and understanding that could be felt throughout the entire community.

In the end, Alex realized that the power of the River of Mindful

Communication wasn't just in the water - it was in the people who were willing to slow down and listen to each other with an open heart and mind.

41

The Path of Transformative Growth: Embracing Change and Stepping Into Your Full Potential.

Once upon a time, there was a young woman named Lily who felt lost and unfulfilled in her life. She had always felt like there was something more for her, but she didn't know what that was or how to find it. Lily knew she needed to make a change but didn't know where to start.

One day, Lily stumbled upon a hiking trail in the mountains near her home. As she walked, she noticed the beauty and serenity of the surroundings. She felt a sense of peace that she had never experienced before. Lily realized that the path she was walking was a metaphor for her life. She needed to step out of her comfort zone and take the path of transformative growth.

Lily started to hike regularly and became more in tune with her body and her surroundings. She felt the fear of the unknown and the exhilaration of pushing herself to new limits. As she gained more confidence, Lily started to explore new hobbies and interests that she had always been curious about.

One day, while on a hike, Lily met a group of women who were all on their own path of growth. They were supportive and encouraging, and they helped Lily to see that she was not alone on her journey. They shared stories of their own challenges and how they overcame them. They gave Lily the courage to keep pushing forward.

With the help of her new friends, Lily started to take risks and try new things. She started a business and enrolled in a course to learn a new skill. She realized that she had always been capable of achieving her dreams but was held back by fear and self-doubt.

As Lily continued on her path of transformative growth, she noticed changes in herself. She felt more confident and self-assured. She was able to handle challenges and setbacks with ease, knowing that they were all part of the journey. Lily became more open-minded and willing to try new things, which led to even more opportunities.

In the end, Lily learned that the path of transformative growth is not always easy, but it is worth it. She found the courage to step out of her comfort zone and embrace change. She learned that growth is a journey, not a destination, and that it is never too late to start. By taking small steps every day, Lily was able to transform her life and become the person she always knew she could be.

42

The Garden of Compassionate Self-Reflection: Learning to Love Yourself Through Honest Examination

Once upon a time, there was a beautiful garden filled with colorful flowers, tall trees, and lush green grass. In the middle of the garden stood a small gazebo where people would come to sit and reflect on their lives.

One day, a woman named Maria visited the garden. She had been feeling unhappy and unfulfilled in her life, and she hoped that the peaceful surroundings would help her find some clarity. As she sat in the gazebo, she began to reflect on her life, and she realized that she had been too hard on herself. She always criticized herself for not being perfect, and this had prevented her from enjoying the simple things in life.

As she walked through the garden, she came across a section

that had been neglected and overgrown with weeds. Maria realized that just like the garden, her life needed some weeding out. She needed to remove the negative thoughts and self-doubt that were holding her back from experiencing joy and happiness.

With this newfound insight, Maria began to make changes in her life. She started a gratitude journal to focus on the positive aspects of her life and to cultivate self-love. She began to practice mindfulness, which helped her to slow down and appreciate the present moment.

As Maria tended to the garden, she realized that just like the plants needed care and attention, so did she. She started to take care of herself by eating healthier and exercising regularly. She also began to connect with others and opened up to the idea of asking for help and support when she needed it.

Slowly but surely, Maria's life began to transform. She started to see the beauty in imperfection and embraced her flaws. She stopped being so hard on herself and learned to love herself unconditionally.

One day, as Maria sat in the gazebo, she looked out at the garden with a sense of contentment and peace. She realized that just like the garden, her life was a work in progress. She would continue to tend to it, pruning the negative and nurturing the positive, as she grew and evolved into the best version of herself.

From that day on, Maria visited the garden often, not just to reflect, but to connect with the beauty of nature and to be reminded of the valuable lesson she had learned – to be kind to herself and to cultivate self-compassion.

43

The Ocean of Empowered Action: Harnessing Your Strength and Taking Bold Steps Toward Your Dreams

I n a small village near the ocean, there lived a young girl named Maya. She had always been fascinated by the sea and dreamed of becoming a sailor one day. However, her family and the villagers discouraged her from pursuing such a dangerous and unconventional career path, telling her that it was not meant for girls like her.

Maya was disheartened by their lack of support but refused to give up on her dream. She spent all her free time studying the art of sailing and building her own small boat, determined to prove everyone wrong.

One day, while out at sea, a fierce storm hit, and Maya's boat was tossed around violently. Despite her fear, she remembered her training and used all her strength and skill to navigate the boat through the storm. Finally, after hours of struggle, she managed to steer the boat to safety.

Exhausted and soaked to the bone, Maya collapsed onto the sand and looked out to the vast ocean. In that moment, she realized that she had the power within herself to overcome any obstacle that came her way. She no longer cared about what others thought of her dream and decided to pursue it with all her might.

Maya spent the next few years honing her sailing skills, and soon she became one of the best sailors in the village. People started to notice her talent and determination and began to support her dream. She even inspired some of the other girls in the village to take up sailing as well.

One day, a wealthy merchant came to the village and offered Maya a job as a sailor on his ship. It was an opportunity of a lifetime, and Maya eagerly accepted. She sailed across the vast ocean, visiting exotic lands and encountering many challenges along the way. But each time, she faced them head-on and emerged even stronger.

Years later, Maya returned to her village as a successful sailor and an inspiration to many. She realized that the ocean had taught her an important lesson: that she had the power within herself to create her own destiny and make her dreams come true.

From that day on, Maya dedicated herself to empowering other young girls in her village to pursue their dreams, no matter how unconventional or challenging they may seem. She knew that the ocean of empowered action was waiting for them, and all they had to do was take the first step towards their dreams.

44

The Mountain of Fearless Adventure: Conquering Doubt and Embracing the Unknown

O nce upon a time, there was a young woman named Mia who lived in a small village at the base of a towering mountain range. Mia had always dreamed of exploring the world beyond her village, but she was held back by her fears and doubts.

One day, Mia met an old adventurer who had climbed the highest peaks and crossed the widest oceans. The adventurer saw the longing in Mia's eyes and offered to take her on a journey to the top of the highest mountain in the range.

Mia was both thrilled and terrified at the prospect, but she decided to seize the opportunity to face her fears and embark on an adventure of a lifetime.

As they began their ascent, Mia felt her heart pounding in her chest and her legs growing weaker with each step. But the adventurer was patient and encouraging, reminding her to take it one step at a time and to trust in herself.

As they climbed higher and higher, the air grew thin, and the winds grew stronger, but Mia refused to give up. She pushed herself further than she ever thought possible, her body and mind fueled by the exhilaration of the climb.

Finally, they reached the summit, and Mia felt a rush of joy and triumph unlike anything she had ever experienced. She looked out at the breathtaking vista before her and felt grateful for having the courage to face her fears and pursue her dreams.

The adventurer smiled at Mia and said, "This mountain may be conquered, but there are always new mountains to climb. And with each one, you will find that the journey is just as important as the destination."

Mia knew then that she had discovered a new passion, a new purpose in life. She returned to her village, inspired and emboldened, and began planning her next adventure.

From that day forward, Mia lived her life fearlessly, always seeking out new challenges and experiences. She never forgot the lessons she learned on that mountain, and she shared them with others, inspiring them to conquer their own fears and embrace the unknown.

And so, Mia became known throughout the land as the fearless adventurer who never gave up, the one who dared to climb the highest mountains and cross the widest oceans, and who showed others that anything is possible with determination and courage.

45

The Circle of Authentic Expression: Sharing Your Unique Voice and Creativity with the World

Once upon a time, there was a young woman named Maya who dreamed of becoming a writer. She had always loved reading books and writing stories, but never had the courage to share her work with others.

Maya's fear of judgment held her back from pursuing her passion. She worried that her writing wasn't good enough, that she would be laughed at, or that people would think she was foolish for trying. So instead of writing, she kept her dreams hidden away and let her talent go to waste.

One day, Maya met an older writer named Ben who was in the process of publishing his first book. They struck up a conversation, and Maya couldn't help but admire Ben's bravery for pursuing his dreams despite the risk of failure.

As they talked, Ben sensed that Maya had a gift for writing and encouraged her to share her work with him.

At first, Maya was hesitant. She had never let anyone read her writing before and feared the rejection that might come with it. But with Ben's gentle encouragement, she decided to take a chance and share one of her stories.

To her surprise, Ben was impressed with her writing. He saw a spark of talent and creativity that was waiting to be unleashed. Maya was overjoyed to receive such positive feedback and felt a newfound sense of confidence.

With Ben's guidance, Maya began to write more and share her work with others. She learned to embrace her unique voice and to express herself authentically through her writing. As she became more comfortable with sharing her work, Maya started to receive recognition and praise for her writing.

Over time, Maya realized that her fear of judgment had been holding her back from living the life she truly wanted. She learned that the only way to truly succeed is to take risks and be true to yourself, even if it means facing criticism and rejection.

Maya's writing not only brought her joy and fulfillment, but it also inspired others to follow their own dreams. She discovered that by sharing her authentic voice with the world, she could make a difference in the lives of others.

In the end, Maya realized that the circle of authentic expression was not just about her writing, but about living a life that was true to herself. She learned that when you have the courage to be authentic, you can inspire others to do the same and make the world a better place.

46

The River of Grateful Giving: Cultivating Generosity and Making a Difference in the Lives of Others

There was once a man named Michael who lived in a small town in the countryside. He was a successful businessman, but he felt unfulfilled in his life. He yearned for something more, something that would give his life meaning beyond his work.

One day, while taking a walk by the river that ran through the town, he saw a group of children playing and laughing. As he watched them, he noticed a young boy sitting alone on the riverbank, watching the others play. Michael approached him and asked why he wasn't playing with the other children.

The boy replied, "I don't have any toys to play with, and my parents can't afford to buy me any."

Michael's heart sank, and he knew he had to do something to help this child and others like him. He decided to organize a toy drive in the town, encouraging people to donate toys for children who couldn't afford them.

To his surprise, the response was overwhelming. People donated toys of all kinds, from dolls and action figures to board games and sports equipment. Michael was touched by the generosity of his fellow townspeople, and he knew he had to do more to help those in need.

He organized a charity auction to raise money for underprivileged families in the town, and it was a huge success. The money raised went towards buying food, clothing, and other essentials for those who were struggling to make ends meet.

As Michael became more involved in helping others, he felt a sense of purpose and fulfillment that he had never experienced before. He realized that he had been given so much in his life, and it was his responsibility to give back to those who were less fortunate.

The toy drive and charity auction became an annual event, and over the years, Michael's efforts grew into a larger non-profit organization that helped families in need throughout the region.

Michael's life had been transformed by the simple act of giving. He had found his true calling in life, and it was not in his successful business, but in his ability to make a difference in the lives of others.

As he watched the children playing with the toys that had been donated, he felt a sense of joy and gratitude that he had never known before. He realized that the river of grateful giving flowed both ways, and that he had received just as much as he had given.

From that day on, Michael knew that his life would be dedicated to giving back to others, and he had found a sense of purpose and fulfillment that he had never known before.

47

The Bridge of Intentional Living: Living with Purpose and Mindful Direction

There was a man named Sam who had spent most of his life going with the flow. He had a job that paid the bills, but he wasn't passionate about it. He had hobbies that he enjoyed, but he never dedicated much time to them. He had relationships that were pleasant, but not deeply fulfilling. Sam felt like he was just going through the motions of life.

One day, while out for a walk, Sam came across a bridge. It was a beautiful bridge, with intricate carvings and a stunning view of the river below. As he crossed the bridge, he couldn't help but feel a sense of purpose and direction that he had never experienced before.

Sam realized that he had been living his life on autopilot,

without any real intention or direction. He had been letting life happen to him, instead of taking charge of his own destiny.

Inspired by the bridge, Sam began to make intentional choices in his life. He started to dedicate more time to his hobbies, and even found a way to turn one of them into a small business. He began to take more risks at work, and soon found himself in a leadership position that he never would have thought possible.

Sam also started to build deeper, more meaningful relationships with the people in his life. He made a point to spend more time with his family and friends, and even started volunteering at a local charity.

As Sam continued to live with intention and purpose, he found that his life became more fulfilling and satisfying. He was no longer just going through the motions, but was actively shaping his own life and creating the future he wanted.

Years went by, and Sam eventually found himself back at the bridge that had changed his life so many years before. As he looked out at the river below, he felt a deep sense of gratitude for the intentional choices he had made, and for the life he had created.

Sam realized that the bridge had been a symbol of the power of intentional living, and that by crossing it, he had set himself on a path that had led him to a life filled with purpose and fulfillment.

From that day forward, Sam made a promise to himself to

always live with intention, and to never let life just happen to him again.

48

The Forest of Mindful Resilience: Strengthening Your Inner Resources and Bouncing Back from Adversity

In the heart of a dense forest, a young woman named Lily wandered aimlessly, feeling lost and overwhelmed. She had just experienced a traumatic event that had left her feeling vulnerable and powerless. As she wandered deeper into the forest, she stumbled upon a clearing where an old tree stood tall and strong.

As she approached the tree, she noticed a group of squirrels playing around the roots, and a family of birds perched on its branches. As she gazed at the magnificent tree, she felt a sense of peace and comfort.

She decided to sit down next to the tree and closed her eyes, taking a deep breath in and out. As she breathed, she felt the energy of the forest flowing through her body. She realized that the forest was a place of healing and that the tree was a symbol of resilience.

As she sat in silence, she began to reflect on the events that had brought her to the forest. She realized that although she couldn't change what had happened, she could choose how she responded to it. She decided that she would not let the trauma define her, but instead, she would use it as a source of strength to help her move forward.

As she opened her eyes, she noticed a small sapling growing at the base of the old tree. It was a symbol of new life and growth. She realized that just as the tree had weathered many storms and continued to stand tall, she too could weather any storm that came her way.

With renewed determination, she stood up and made her way back through the forest. As she walked, she felt a sense of purpose and resilience that she had never felt before. She knew that life would present her with challenges, but she also knew that she had the inner resources to overcome them.

From that day forward, Lily spent more time in the forest, using it as a source of inspiration and renewal. She learned that just as the forest was home to many different species of plants and animals, each with their unique strengths and abilities, she too had her unique strengths and abilities that made her who she was.

Lily's experience in the forest taught her the power of mindful resilience, the ability to bounce back from adversity with renewed strength and purpose. She learned that just as the old tree had weathered many storms and continued to thrive, she too could thrive in the face of adversity.

49

The Path of Radiant Positivity: Choosing Joy and Spreading Light in the World

Once upon a time, there was a young girl named Lily who lived in a small village at the foot of a beautiful mountain. Despite her humble surroundings, Lily was a bright and cheerful girl who always looked on the bright side of life. She loved to spend her days playing with her friends, helping her family with chores, and exploring the lush forests around her village.

One day, Lily heard about a mystical path that led to the top of the mountain, where it was said that one could find eternal happiness and bliss. She became obsessed with the idea of finding this path and embarking on a journey to the top of the mountain.

Determined to find the path, Lily set out on a long and

challenging trek through the forest. As she walked, she encountered many obstacles and setbacks, from steep cliffs to treacherous streams. But she remained undaunted, always keeping her sights on the top of the mountain and the promise of eternal happiness.

Finally, after many days of traveling, Lily stumbled upon the path she had been seeking. It was narrow and winding, and she could see that it would be a difficult climb to the top. But with her unflagging spirit, Lily began to make her way up the path.

As she climbed, she encountered many other travelers who were also making their way up the mountain. Some were grumpy and complaining, while others were tired and discouraged. But Lily remained cheerful and positive, always offering a kind word or a smile to those she met.

Eventually, Lily reached the top of the mountain, where she found a beautiful garden filled with flowers and sunshine. She felt a deep sense of peace and joy wash over her, and she knew that she had finally found the happiness she had been seeking.

As she looked around, Lily saw that many other travelers had also made it to the top of the mountain. Some were still grumpy and complaining, while others were now smiling and laughing. Lily realized that the happiness she had found was not just for her, but for everyone who had made the journey to the top.

From that day forward, Lily made it her mission to spread

positivity and joy wherever she went. She knew that the path to happiness was not an easy one, but she also knew that with a positive attitude and a kind heart, anything was possible. And so she walked back down the mountain, ready to continue her journey of spreading light and love in the world.

50

The Circle of Joyful Connection: Building Supportive and Uplifting Relationships with Others

Once upon a time, there was a woman named Emily who lived in a small town. Emily was friendly and kind, but she always felt like something was missing in her life. She had a good job, a comfortable home, and a loving family, but she didn't feel truly connected to anyone in her community.

One day, Emily decided to join a local group that met regularly to do volunteer work and support each other's goals. At first, she was nervous about putting herself out there and meeting new people, but she quickly realized that everyone in the group was just as kind and genuine as she was.

Over the weeks and months that followed, Emily found herself becoming more and more involved in the group's activities.

She helped to organize charity events, attended workshops on personal development, and even went on a few group outings with her new friends.

As she spent more time with the group, Emily began to notice a profound shift in her life. She felt happier, more fulfilled, and more confident than ever before. She realized that the joy she had been seeking was not something she could find on her own, but something she could only experience through meaningful connections with others.

One day, Emily was walking through town when she ran into an old acquaintance who she hadn't seen in years. The woman looked tired and sad, and Emily felt a pang of empathy for her. Without thinking, she invited the woman to join her and her friends at their next group meeting.

To Emily's surprise, the woman showed up the following week, and she seemed genuinely touched by the warmth and support of the group. Over time, she began to open up and share her own struggles, and Emily watched as the other members of the group rallied around her and lifted her up.

As Emily looked around the room at her new friends, she felt overwhelmed with gratitude and joy. She knew that she had found something truly special in this group of people who had come together to support and uplift one another. And she knew that she would always cherish these connections and the joy they brought to her life.

51

The Garden of Mindful Leadership: Inspiring and Empowering Others Through Authenticity and Compassion.

Once upon a time, there was a successful businesswoman named Maya who had climbed the corporate ladder through hard work, intelligence, and a fierce determination to succeed. She had always been ambitious and driven, but she noticed that as she advanced in her career, she became more isolated from her team and less connected to the values that had originally inspired her.

One day, while on a business trip to Japan, Maya had the opportunity to visit a traditional Japanese garden. As she strolled through the serene pathways and admired the meticulously manicured plants, she felt a sense of calm and clarity that had eluded her for years.

As she sat on a bench overlooking a koi pond, Maya realized that she had lost touch with her own values and purpose in her pursuit of success. She had become so focused on achieving her goals and meeting deadlines that she had forgotten the importance of leading with compassion, empathy, and authenticity.

Maya returned from her trip with a newfound sense of purpose and a desire to become a more mindful leader. She began to take the time to listen to her team members, to empathize with their concerns, and to lead by example. She started to encourage creativity and collaboration, fostering an environment of open communication and trust.

As Maya implemented these changes, she noticed a shift in the energy of the workplace. Her team members felt heard, supported, and empowered to bring their best selves to work. They began to work together more cohesively, and the company started to achieve even greater success than before.

Maya's transformation as a leader was not easy, and there were certainly moments of doubt and fear along the way. But she remained committed to her values and her intention to lead with compassion and authenticity. She recognized that true leadership requires not only intelligence and hard work, but also self-awareness, empathy, and a willingness to learn and grow.

As she sat in her office one day, reflecting on her journey, Maya felt a sense of deep gratitude and contentment. She realized that her success was not just measured by her achievements, but also by the impact she had on others. She felt a sense of joy knowing that she was making a positive difference in the lives of her team members and inspiring them to be their best selves.

Maya continued to lead with mindfulness and compassion, and her company thrived under her leadership. She became known as a respected and beloved leader, and her legacy inspired countless others to lead with intention and authenticity.

52

The Path of Grateful Abundance: Seeing the Beauty in Life's Simple Moments

Once upon a time, there was a man named Jack who lived a simple life in a small village. He was content with what he had, but he always dreamed of having more. He believed that he would be happy only if he had a big house, a fancy car, and a lot of money.

One day, Jack decided to take a walk in the nearby forest. As he was walking, he saw a beautiful butterfly flying around. He followed the butterfly, and it led him to a small clearing in the woods. In the center of the clearing was a beautiful garden filled with colorful flowers, lush greenery, and fruit trees.

As Jack was admiring the garden, an old man appeared. The old man introduced himself as the keeper of the garden and invited Jack to take a closer look. Jack was amazed at the beauty and abundance of the garden. He asked the old man how he could have such a beautiful garden like this.

The old man smiled and said, "It's all about being grateful for what you have. This garden thrives because I take care of it with love and gratitude. I appreciate every moment I spend here, and I am thankful for the abundance that it brings."

Jack realized that he had been so focused on what he didn't have that he had forgotten to be grateful for what he did have. He began to reflect on the simple moments in his life that he had overlooked. He realized that he had a loving family, good health, and a beautiful village to live in. He felt a sense of gratitude and contentment fill his heart.

As he left the garden, the old man handed him a seed and said, "Plant this seed in your heart, and water it with gratitude every day. Soon, you will see the beauty and abundance in your life."

Jack went back to his village and started to practice gratitude every day. He realized that he didn't need a big house, a fancy car, or a lot of money to be happy. He found joy in the simple moments of life like spending time with his family, taking walks in nature, and helping his neighbors.

As time went by, Jack's life changed for the better. He became a happier person, and people around him noticed the change. His positive attitude and grateful heart inspired others to appreciate the simple moments in life.

From that day on, Jack became known as the happiest person

in the village, and his life was filled with grateful abundance.

53

The Circle of Fearless Vulnerability: Embracing the Unknown with Courage and Openness

There was once a young woman named Maya who had always played it safe in life. She never took any risks or pursued her dreams because she was too afraid of failure and rejection. Maya had a comfortable life, but deep down, she knew she was missing out on something more fulfilling.

One day, Maya stumbled upon a workshop that promised to help participants overcome their fears and become more courageous. She signed up, hoping it would give her the push she needed to break out of her shell.

The workshop was held in a small, cozy room, and there were about a dozen people in attendance. They were all strangers to each other, but they had one thing in common: they wanted to step out of their comfort zones and face their fears head-on.

The facilitator began by explaining that fear was a natural part of life and that everyone experiences it at some point. She encouraged the participants to embrace their fears and to be vulnerable with each other. Maya felt a knot in her stomach as she listened, but she also felt a glimmer of hope.

The first exercise was simple. Each person had to share something they were afraid of. Maya was nervous, but when it was her turn, she took a deep breath and spoke from the heart. She talked about how she had always dreamed of starting her own business but was too afraid to take the leap.

To her surprise, the other participants were supportive and encouraging. They shared their own fears and struggles, and Maya realized that she wasn't alone. They even brainstormed ideas for her business and offered to help her get started.

As the workshop continued, Maya found herself opening up more and more. She shared stories about her childhood, her hopes and dreams, and her fears. Each time, she felt a little bit braver, and each time, the group rallied around her with love and support.

By the end of the workshop, Maya felt like a different person. She had faced her fears head-on and had come out stronger on the other side. She had also made some amazing new friends who she knew would be there for her no matter what.

As Maya left the workshop, she felt a renewed sense of courage and a deep gratitude for the people who had shared the journey with her. She realized that being vulnerable wasn't a weakness, but rather, it was a strength that allowed her to connect with others and to live a more authentic life. From that day forward, she promised herself that she would embrace her fears and be fearless in her vulnerability.

54

The River of Mindful Parenting: Raising Children with Compassion and Presence

Once upon a time, there was a mother who was always busy, always rushing from one task to another. She loved her children dearly, but she found it hard to find the time to really connect with them. One day, feeling overwhelmed and exhausted, she decided to take her children on a walk along the riverbank.

As they walked, her mind raced with all the things she needed to do when they got home. She hardly noticed the beauty of the river, the way the sun sparkled on the water, and the birds singing in the trees. Her children, however, were fascinated by every little thing they saw, the sound of the water, the shape of the leaves on the trees, and the bugs crawling on the ground.

The mother noticed how present her children were, how they

were truly in the moment, and how happy they seemed. She realized that her children had something to teach her about being mindful and present. She took a deep breath and decided to let go of her worries and be present with her children.

They stopped to watch a group of ducks paddling in the river, and the mother showed her children how to skip stones across the water. They laughed and played, and for a moment, the mother forgot about all her worries and responsibilities. As they walked back home, she felt a sense of peace and contentment she hadn't felt in a long time.

From that day on, the mother made an effort to be more present with her children, to listen to them, and to really see them. She learned to slow down and appreciate the small moments of joy in life. She found that being mindful helped her be a better parent, and that her children responded to her presence with more love and affection.

Years later, when her children were grown, they would look back on that walk along the river as one of their favorite memories with their mother. They remembered how happy and carefree she seemed, and how much they loved spending time with her. The mother was grateful for that moment of realization by the river, that helped her be a more mindful and present parent, and to create memories that would last a lifetime.

55

The Garden of Mindful Eating: Nourishing Your Body and Soul with Consciousness and Gratitude

Once upon a time, there was a woman named Sarah who struggled with her relationship with food. She had spent most of her life yo-yo dieting and obsessing over her weight, constantly swinging from feeling guilty after indulging in her favorite foods to feeling deprived when she restricted herself too much.

One day, Sarah decided she had had enough. She wanted to break free from this cycle of self-punishment and find a healthier relationship with food. She knew it wouldn't be easy, but she was determined to make a change.

Sarah started by researching and learning about mindful eating. She discovered that it wasn't just about what she ate, but how she ate. Mindful eating was about being present in the moment and savoring every bite, paying attention to her body's hunger and fullness signals, and approaching food with a sense of curiosity and gratitude.

At first, it was a challenge for Sarah to slow down and really focus on her food. She was used to mindlessly scarfing down her meals while scrolling through social media or watching TV. But as she practiced, she began to notice a shift in her attitude towards food.

She found herself feeling more appreciative of the flavors and textures of her meals, and even started experimenting with new recipes and ingredients. She also noticed that she felt more satisfied and energized after eating, without the guilt or shame she had experienced before.

As Sarah continued to practice mindful eating, she began to see other positive changes in her life. She started to feel more in tune with her body, and was able to recognize when she was actually hungry versus when she was eating out of boredom or stress. She also became more compassionate towards herself, recognizing that her worth was not tied to her weight or appearance.

Through her journey with mindful eating, Sarah discovered a new sense of freedom and joy in her relationship with food. She realized that nourishing her body wasn't just about the physical act of eating, but about cultivating a deeper appreciation for the abundance and beauty of life. And she was grateful for every moment she spent enjoying the flavors and nourishment of her meals, savoring each bite with a sense of mindfulness and gratitude.

56

The Mountain of Unconditional Love: Embracing and Accepting Others Without Judgment

Once upon a time, in a small village nestled in the mountains, there lived an old wise woman. She was known for her kindness and compassion towards others. Everyone in the village respected her and sought her advice whenever they needed it.

One day, a young couple came to her for guidance. They were newly married and deeply in love. However, they were facing challenges in their relationship. The wife was struggling with accepting her husband's flaws, and the husband was finding it hard to be himself around her.

The old wise woman listened to their problems patiently and then said, "My dear children, love is not about perfection. It's about accepting someone wholeheartedly, flaws and all.

It's about seeing the beauty in the imperfections and loving someone unconditionally."

She then took them on a journey up the mountain, to the top of the peak. As they walked, she told them stories of the different people she had met in her life and how she had learned to love them despite their imperfections. She spoke of the importance of understanding and empathy.

Finally, they reached the top of the mountain, and the old wise woman pointed to the breathtaking view of the valley below. She said, "Look at this beautiful view. Can you see how everything comes together perfectly? The trees, the river, the sky, and the mountains. Each element is unique and imperfect, yet together they create this magnificent scene."

The young couple looked at each other and then at the view, and they understood what the old wise woman was trying to tell them. They realized that their love was like the view from the mountain. They were imperfect, but together they were beautiful.

They went back to the village with a renewed sense of understanding and compassion. They learned to accept each other's flaws and love each other unconditionally. They also began to appreciate the imperfections in others and treat everyone with kindness and empathy.

The old wise woman's teachings had transformed their relationship and their lives. They knew that true love was not about finding someone perfect but about loving someone perfectly, flaws and all.

From that day on, the young couple made it a point to climb the mountain every year to remind themselves of the old wise woman's teachings and to renew their commitment to each other. And every time they reached the top, they looked out at the valley below and marveled at the beauty of imperfection.

57

The Path of Empowered Self-Care: Prioritizing Your Well-Being and Happiness

Once upon a time, there was a woman named Maya who was always busy taking care of everyone around her. She was a loving mother, a supportive wife, and a dependable friend. However, she neglected to take care of herself and her own needs.

Maya woke up early every morning to make breakfast for her family, pack lunches, and get her kids ready for school. Then, she rushed to work where she spent long hours at her desk, barely taking breaks for herself. After work, Maya would pick up her kids from school, drive them to their extracurricular activities, and then come home to make dinner for her family. By the end of the day, she was exhausted and had no energy left for herself.

One day, Maya's best friend invited her for a weekend getaway to a nearby spa. At first, Maya hesitated to accept the invitation, feeling guilty for taking time off from her responsibilities. But, her friend insisted that Maya deserved a break and needed to take care of herself.

The spa was a serene and calming place. Maya was amazed at how relaxed she felt just being there. She indulged in massages, facials, and spent time in the sauna and hot tub. For once, she didn't have to worry about anyone else but herself. Maya felt grateful for the opportunity to unwind and recharge her batteries.

As she sat in the hot tub, gazing up at the stars, Maya realized that she needed to make a change. She couldn't keep going on like this, neglecting her own well-being. When she returned home, she decided to make a few changes to her routine. She started taking short breaks during the day to meditate or take a walk. She hired a babysitter for a few hours each week so that she could have some time to herself. Maya also started attending a yoga class, which she found to be a relaxing and rejuvenating experience.

Over time, Maya noticed that she had more energy, felt happier, and was able to be more present for her family and friends. She realized that taking care of herself was not selfish but was actually necessary for her own well-being and the well-being of those around her. Maya had learned that self-care was not just a luxury but a crucial aspect of living a fulfilling life.

From that day on, Maya made a commitment to prioritize her own self-care, knowing that it would lead to a happier and healthier life.

58

The Ocean of Limitless Possibilities: Embracing Your Inner Potential and Dreaming Big

Once upon a time, there was a young woman named Maya who lived by the ocean. She had always been fascinated by the vastness and mystery of the sea, and often found herself lost in daydreams of what lay beyond the horizon. But Maya had also been taught to be practical and cautious, and so she kept her feet firmly planted on the shore.

One day, while taking a walk on the beach, Maya stumbled upon a small boat that had washed up on the sand. It was old and weathered, but still sturdy enough to set sail. As she looked at it, a wild thought crossed her mind – what if she took the boat and ventured out into the open sea, to explore and discover new places?

At first, Maya dismissed the idea as foolish and impractical. But as days went by, she found that she couldn't stop thinking about it. It was like a seed had been planted in her mind, and it was starting to grow.

One morning, Maya woke up early, packed some food and water, and headed to the beach. The boat was still there, waiting for her. Without further hesitation, she pushed it into the water, jumped in, and set sail.

As she moved farther and farther from the shore, Maya felt a mix of exhilaration and fear. What if she got lost, or ran into a storm? What if she never found her way back home? But she also felt a sense of freedom and possibility that she had never experienced before. She was in control of her own destiny, and the horizon was her only limit.

Days turned into weeks, and weeks turned into months. Maya explored new islands, met new people, and had adventures she had never imagined possible. She faced storms and dangerous sea creatures, but also witnessed the most stunning sunsets and starry skies. And through it all, she discovered something about herself – that she was stronger and braver than she ever knew.

Eventually, Maya returned to the shore, changed by her experience. She knew that she could never go back to her old life of playing it safe and following the rules. Instead, she would continue to explore and dream big, knowing that the ocean of life held limitless possibilities for those who dared to set sail.

From that day on, Maya lived her life with a sense of purpose and adventure, always looking for new opportunities to grow and learn. And as she looked out at the vast expanse of the ocean, she smiled, knowing that anything was possible for those who were willing to take the risk and chase their dreams.

59

The Bridge of Resilient Forgiveness: Letting Go of Grudges and Moving Forward with Grace

O nce there was a young woman named Rachel who had experienced a traumatic event that left her feeling angry, hurt, and betrayed. She couldn't shake off the resentment she felt towards the person who had caused her pain, and the bitterness consumed her every waking moment. She wanted to move on from the past, but she couldn't find it in herself to forgive.

One day, Rachel went on a walk and stumbled upon an old bridge that overlooked a beautiful river. As she stood there, she noticed a piece of paper that was tucked into one of the railings. Curiosity got the best of her, and she reached over to grab it. To her surprise, it was a message that read: "Forgiveness is the bridge that leads to peace."

Rachel couldn't shake off the feeling that the message was meant for her. She knew deep down that she needed to find a way to let go of her anger and forgive the person who had hurt her. Over the next few weeks, Rachel spent a lot of time on the bridge, reflecting on her life and her emotions. She started to realize that holding on to her anger was only hurting herself, and that forgiveness was the key to her own inner peace.

One day, Rachel mustered up the courage to confront the person who had hurt her. She didn't know what the outcome would be, but she knew that she needed to try. To her surprise, the person was genuinely remorseful and apologized for the pain they had caused. Rachel felt a weight lifted off her shoulders, and she knew that she had made the right choice in forgiving.

From that moment on, Rachel started to see the world through a different lens. She no longer held onto grudges, and she let go of the anger that had consumed her for so long. She found herself feeling more at peace, and she even started to see beauty in the world around her. She realized that forgiveness was not only a gift to the person she forgave, but it was also a gift to herself.

Rachel continued to visit the bridge, and she even started to leave her own messages of hope and forgiveness for others to find. She knew that if the message on the paper had helped her, it could help others too. And so, the bridge became a symbol of resilient forgiveness, a place where people could come to let go of their grudges and find peace.

Rachel realized that the power of forgiveness was not just in the act of forgiving, but also in the healing that it brought to her own heart. She learned that forgiving didn't mean forgetting, but it meant letting go of the pain and moving forward with grace.

60

The Circle of Courageous Authenticity: Embracing Your True Self and Finding Confidence in Vulnerability

Once upon a time, in a small village, there was a young girl named Lily. Lily was known for being shy and introverted, always afraid of expressing her true thoughts and feelings to others. She was constantly worried about what others would think of her, so she kept to herself most of the time.

One day, Lily decided that she was tired of living a life filled with fear and decided to take a chance. She wanted to express her true self and embrace her unique qualities, no matter what others may think. So, she set out on a journey to find her inner courage and authenticity.

As she walked along the path, she came across a wise old

woman who had lived in the village for many years. Lily approached the woman and shared her struggle with finding the courage to be her authentic self. The wise old woman smiled warmly and shared her own story of overcoming fear and embracing her true self.

She told Lily that it takes great courage to be vulnerable and show your true self to the world. But by doing so, you inspire others to do the same, and in turn, create a community of courageous authenticity.

Lily was inspired by the wise old woman's words and decided to take action. She began to slowly open up to those around her, sharing her thoughts and feelings without fear of judgment. To her surprise, she found that people began to appreciate her honesty and vulnerability.

As she continued on her journey, Lily found that the more she embraced her true self, the more confident and empowered she became. She felt a newfound sense of freedom and joy that she had never experienced before.

Eventually, Lily returned to her village, no longer afraid to express her authentic self. She found that by embracing her true self, she had created meaningful connections with others and had become a source of inspiration for those around her.

From that day on, Lily lived her life with courage and authenticity, never letting fear hold her back again. She had found the strength to embrace her true self and inspire others to do the same, creating a circle of courageous authenticity that would continue to grow and flourish for years to come.

61

The Forest of Mindful Boundaries: Creating Healthy Relationships Through Self-Respect and Communication

I n the heart of the forest, there lived a family of deer. Among them was a young fawn named Lily who loved exploring her surroundings. One day, while wandering through the woods, she stumbled upon a small clearing where a group of rabbits were having a picnic.

Feeling curious, Lily approached the rabbits and introduced herself. They welcomed her with open arms and invited her to join them for some delicious carrot cake. As they chatted and laughed, Lily noticed that one of the rabbits, named Benny, seemed uncomfortable and nervous.

Concerned, Lily asked Benny if everything was okay. At first, he hesitated to speak, but eventually confided in her that he was being bullied by some of the other rabbits in his community. They made fun of him for being different and teased him about his appearance.

Lily listened attentively and offered her support, telling Benny that she believed in him and that he was special just the way he was. Inspired by her words, Benny felt a newfound sense of courage and decided to stand up to his bullies.

The next day, Lily went back to the clearing and was thrilled to find Benny there waiting for her, smiling from ear to ear. He told her that he had confronted his bullies and stood up for himself, and that he felt empowered and proud of who he was.

From that day forward, Lily and Benny became the best of friends, and Lily taught Benny the importance of setting healthy boundaries and standing up for oneself. Together, they explored the forest, making new friends and spreading positivity wherever they went.

As they journeyed through the woods, they encountered many animals who had experienced similar struggles with bullies or difficult relationships. With Lily's guidance, they learned how to communicate their needs effectively and create healthy boundaries, building stronger and more fulfilling connections with those around them.

Through her kind and compassionate nature, Lily had created a safe space in the forest where animals could come together, support one another, and grow stronger as a community. She showed them that true strength comes from within and that setting healthy boundaries is essential to living a happy and fulfilling life.

As Lily and Benny looked out over the forest, they felt grateful for the beautiful connections they had made and the powerful lessons they had learned. They knew that with their newfound resilience and courage, they could tackle any challenge that lay ahead and continue to create a world filled with love, kindness, and compassion.

62

The Mountain of Relentless Perseverance: Overcoming Challenges with Grit and Determination

In a small village nestled at the foot of a great mountain, there lived a young boy named Taro. Taro had always dreamed of climbing the mountain and reaching the summit, but it seemed like an impossible feat. The mountain was treacherous, and many had attempted to climb it before, but none had ever made it to the top.

Despite the warnings of the elders in the village, Taro refused to give up on his dream. He trained every day, running up and down the steep hills surrounding the village, and practicing his rock-climbing skills.

One day, Taro set out to climb the mountain. The climb was long and grueling, and he faced many obstacles along the way.

He slipped on loose rocks, stumbled over roots, and fought through dense patches of brush. But Taro never lost sight of his goal.

As he climbed higher and higher, the air grew thinner, and the winds stronger. Taro felt his muscles burning and his lungs gasping for air, but he pushed through the pain and continued climbing.

Finally, after many hours of climbing, Taro reached the summit of the mountain. He stood at the top, gazing out at the breathtaking view before him, feeling a sense of accomplishment and pride that he had never felt before.

But Taro knew that the climb down the mountain would be just as difficult as the climb up. He took a deep breath, summoning all the strength and determination he had within him, and began his descent.

The journey down was just as treacherous as the climb up, and Taro faced new challenges that he had not anticipated. But he persevered, taking one step at a time, and eventually, he made it safely back to the village.

Word of Taro's incredible feat spread quickly throughout the village, and soon, he became a source of inspiration for many. People would often ask him how he managed to climb the mountain, and he would always respond with a simple answer:

"It was not easy, but I never gave up. I kept pushing forward, even when it seemed impossible. And in the end, I accomplished my goal."

Taro's relentless perseverance had not only allowed him to reach the summit of the mountain but had also taught him a valuable lesson: with determination and hard work, anything is possible.

63

The Path of Courageous Vulnerability: Authenticity as a Path to Connection and Growth

Once upon a time, there was a young woman named Lily. She had always felt like an outsider, never quite fitting in with any particular group. Growing up, she had tried to hide her quirks and flaws, wanting to be seen as perfect by everyone around her. As she got older, she realized that this way of living was exhausting and unfulfilling.

One day, Lily stumbled upon a book about vulnerability. It talked about the power of authenticity and how true connection can only happen when we show our true selves to others. Intrigued, Lily began to explore the idea of vulnerability and what it could mean for her life.

She started small, sharing her thoughts and feelings with a close friend. It was scary at first, but as she saw how her friend responded with understanding and acceptance, she began to feel a sense of relief and freedom. Lily realized that by being vulnerable, she was no longer hiding behind a façade and was allowing others to truly see her.

As Lily continued to practice vulnerability, she found that her relationships became deeper and more meaningful. She was no longer afraid to express her opinions or share her passions with others. She even started to embrace her quirks and flaws, realizing that they were a part of what made her unique and special.

One day, Lily was asked to speak in front of a large group of people about her experiences with vulnerability. She was nervous, but knew that this was an opportunity to inspire others to embrace their own authenticity. As she stood on stage, she spoke from her heart, sharing her struggles and triumphs with vulnerability. To her surprise, she received a standing ovation and was inundated with people thanking her for her courage and honesty.

From that moment on, Lily knew that vulnerability was her path to true connection and growth. She continued to practice it in all areas of her life, whether it was at work, with her family, or in her community. By being her authentic self, she found that she was able to inspire and uplift others to do the same.

In the end, Lily learned that courage and vulnerability go hand in hand. It takes courage to show our true selves to the world, but the rewards are immeasurable. When we are authentic, we allow others to see us for who we truly are, and in doing so, we create deeper connections and a more meaningful life.

64

The Ocean of Compassionate Service: Making a Difference Through Acts of Kindness and Generosity

Once upon a time, there was a small fishing village by the ocean. The people of the village were simple, but they were kind-hearted and always willing to lend a helping hand to their neighbors. One day, a massive storm hit the village, destroying many of their homes and leaving them without food and shelter.

The people of the village were devastated and didn't know what to do. But then, one of the villagers named Kira had an idea. She gathered a group of volunteers and organized a relief effort to help those in need. They went door to door, asking if anyone needed assistance and providing them with food, blankets, and shelter.

As the days passed, more and more people came to Kira and

her team for help. Despite the challenges, Kira refused to give up. She and her team worked tirelessly day and night, putting their own needs aside to ensure that everyone in the village was taken care of.

Slowly but surely, the village began to recover. The people were filled with gratitude for Kira and her team, and they couldn't thank them enough for their selfless acts of kindness. The village was forever changed by the compassion and generosity that Kira and her team had shown.

Kira's actions inspired others to follow in her footsteps. People began to volunteer their time and resources to help those in need. The village became a place of love and compassion, where everyone looked out for one another.

As Kira looked out at the village, she felt a sense of pride and contentment. She had discovered that there was no greater joy than serving others with compassion and kindness. She had learned that even in the darkest of times, there was always hope and that with perseverance, anything was possible.

From that day on, Kira made a promise to herself to always be of service to others. She knew that there was nothing more fulfilling than making a positive difference in someone's life, and she was grateful for the opportunity to do so.

The village had been transformed by the ocean of compassion-ate service that Kira had started. And even though there were still challenges ahead, the people knew that they could count on each other for support and that they would always be there to lend a helping hand to those in need.

65

The Circle of Mindful Gratitude: Cultivating Appreciation for Life's Blessings

In a small village, there lived a young girl named Leila. She was known for her kind and gentle nature, and everyone in the village loved her. One day, Leila was walking by the river when she saw an old man struggling to carry a heavy load of firewood. Without hesitation, she went over to the man and offered to help him carry the load.

The old man was grateful for her help, and as they walked, he asked Leila what her secret to happiness was. She smiled and said, "I try to find something to be grateful for every day. It could be something as small as a beautiful flower or a kind word from a friend."

The old man nodded thoughtfully, and they continued walking in silence until they reached the old man's house. As a thank you for her help, the old man gave Leila a small seed and said, "Plant this seed in your garden and take care of it. You'll know what to do when the time is right."

Leila thanked the old man and went home, excited to plant the seed. She carefully dug a hole in her garden and placed the seed inside, covering it with soil and watering it. Every day, she tended to the seed, making sure it had enough water and sunlight.

Weeks passed, and the seed finally sprouted, revealing a small plant with green leaves. Leila was thrilled and continued to take care of the plant, watching it grow taller and stronger each day.

One morning, Leila woke up to find a beautiful flower blooming on the plant. She gasped in awe at its vibrant colors and sweet fragrance. Overwhelmed with gratitude, Leila realized that the old man's gift was a symbol of the power of gratitude and taking care of something with love.

From that day on, Leila made a habit of finding something to be grateful for each day, and her garden became a sanctuary of beauty and love. People from all over the village came to admire her garden and to learn the secret of her happiness.

Leila's garden had become a symbol of the circle of mindful gratitude, a place where people could come to connect with the power of gratitude and the beauty of nature. And as for Leila, she continued to tend to her garden, knowing that every seed she planted and every flower that bloomed was a testament to the power of gratitude and the joy it brought to her life.

66

The Forest of Creative Flow: Tapping into Your Inner Creativity to Find Joy and Fulfillment

Once upon a time, there was a young woman named Maya who had a passion for painting. She had always loved art and would spend hours creating beautiful pieces that spoke to her soul. However, as she grew older, she found herself becoming busier and more distracted by the demands of everyday life. She was so consumed with work and responsibilities that she barely had any time left for her beloved hobby.

One day, Maya found herself walking through a dense forest, feeling lost and disconnected from herself. She stumbled upon a beautiful glade, bathed in sunlight, and decided to take a moment to rest. As she sat there, she noticed a group of butterflies fluttering around her, their wings aglow in the sunlight.

Maya watched them for a while, mesmerized by their beauty and grace. She realized that just like the butterflies, she too had a unique beauty within her that needed to be expressed. She realized that her passion for painting was an integral part of who she was, and that she needed to find a way to make time for it.

With renewed determination, Maya went home and cleared out a space in her apartment to set up her art supplies. She began to paint every day, even if it was just for a few minutes. Over time, she found herself becoming more and more absorbed in her art, and the stress and worry of her daily life started to melt away.

As she continued to paint, Maya discovered a newfound sense of joy and fulfillment. She found that her creative energy was a powerful force that she could tap into whenever she needed to feel more grounded and connected to herself.

One day, Maya decided to share her artwork with others, and she organized an art exhibit at a local coffee shop. Her paintings were a hit, and people were drawn to the vibrant colors and intricate designs. Maya felt a sense of pride and satisfaction that she had never experienced before, knowing that her creativity had touched the lives of others.

From that day forward, Maya continued to paint, and she found that the more she created, the more ideas and inspiration flowed to her. She realized that creativity was not just a hobby, but a way of life, and that she could use it to connect with others and spread joy and beauty in the world.

And so, Maya continued to paint, tapping into the forest of creative flow within her, and inspiring others to do the same.

67

The Bridge of Conscious Communication: Using Words Wisely to Build Stronger Relationships

O nce upon a time, in a small village nestled among the hills, there lived a man named David. David was well-known in the village for his excellent communication skills and his ability to bring people together. He was often called upon to mediate disputes between families, friends, and even strangers.

One day, a traveler passing through the village approached David and asked for his help. The traveler had been involved in a heated argument with a local shopkeeper over the price of some goods, and the situation had quickly escalated to the point where both parties were shouting and threatening each other.

David listened to the traveler's story and then made his way to the shopkeeper's store. He approached the shopkeeper and asked to hear his side of the story. The shopkeeper was hesitant at first, but David's calm and gentle manner soon put him at ease, and he began to speak.

David listened attentively to the shopkeeper's account of what had happened, and then he asked a few questions to clarify some details. He then turned to the traveler and repeated the shopkeeper's version of events.

To David's surprise, the traveler didn't become angry or defensive. Instead, he nodded thoughtfully and acknowledged that there may have been a misunderstanding. David continued to act as a mediator between the two parties, and eventually, they were able to reach a compromise that satisfied both sides.

As David walked back to his home, he thought about the power of communication. He realized that it wasn't just about being able to speak well or make a good argument. Communication was about truly listening to others, understanding their perspective, and finding common ground.

David began to teach these principles to others in the village, holding workshops and seminars on effective communication. People began to see the value of listening and understanding, and the village became a more harmonious and peaceful place.

Years passed, and David became an old man. He knew that his time was coming to an end, and he wanted to pass on his wisdom to the next generation. He called together a group of young people in the village and shared with them his teachings on communication.

He urged them to always approach others with an open mind and a willingness to listen. He reminded them that every person has their own unique perspective and that it's only by working together and communicating effectively that we can build stronger, more loving relationships.

The young people listened intently to David's words, and they left feeling inspired and empowered. They went out into the world, spreading David's teachings and building bridges between people of all backgrounds and cultures.

David passed away shortly after that meeting, but his legacy lived on. His teachings continued to inspire and guide people for generations to come, reminding them of the power of conscious communication to create stronger, more connected communities.

68

The River of Resilient Hope: Finding Strength in the Face of Adversity

Once upon a time, there was a young woman named Lily who had a heart full of hope. She had always been a dreamer and believed in the power of positive thinking, even when life was difficult.

One day, Lily's world was turned upside down when her mother was diagnosed with a serious illness. It was a difficult time for Lily and her family, and it was hard to stay hopeful when faced with such a challenge.

As the weeks went by, Lily watched her mother struggle with her illness, but she also saw how her mother held onto hope and refused to give up. Despite the difficulties, her mother remained optimistic and determined to fight.

Lily was inspired by her mother's resilience and decided to adopt the same mindset. She realized that hope was not just a feeling, but an active choice she could make every day.

So, Lily started to focus on the good things in her life and the things that brought her joy. She spent more time with her family, went for walks in nature, and started a gratitude journal where she wrote down things she was thankful for each day.

Even though her mother's illness was still present, Lily found that the more she focused on the positive things in her life, the more hope she felt. She started to see possibilities where she had previously only seen obstacles.

One day, Lily's mother received news that her treatment was working, and there was hope for recovery. The news brought tears of joy to Lily's eyes, and she knew that her mother's resilience and determination had paid off.

From that day forward, Lily made a promise to herself to always choose hope, even when life was hard. She knew that hope was not just a feeling but a powerful force that could carry her through difficult times.

Years later, when Lily faced challenges of her own, she remembered the lessons her mother had taught her about hope and resilience. She leaned into her own inner strength and found the courage to persevere.

Lily learned that hope was not a naive belief that everything would work out perfectly, but a courageous decision to believe in a brighter future, even when the present was difficult.

Through her own experiences, Lily became a beacon of hope for others, showing them that even in the darkest of times, hope could be found and that with resilience and determination, anything was possible.

69

The Garden of Intentional Relationships: Nurturing Meaningful Connections with Others

In the heart of a bustling city, there was a small garden tucked away from the chaos and noise of the world. It was a place where people came to escape the hustle and bustle and find a moment of peace and tranquility. One day, a woman named Sarah stumbled upon the garden by chance. She had been feeling lonely and disconnected from others and was looking for a way to connect with the world around her.

As she walked through the garden, she noticed a group of people sitting in a circle, deep in conversation. She approached them hesitantly, unsure if she should intrude. But the group welcomed her warmly and invited her to join them. They introduced themselves as members of a community dedicated to intentional relationships - the art of nurturing deep and meaningful connections with others.

Sarah was intrigued. She had always struggled with forming meaningful relationships and was looking for a way to connect with others in a more authentic way. The group invited her to attend their weekly meetings, where they would explore different ways to build and maintain intentional relationships.

At the first meeting, the group discussed the importance of listening with empathy and being fully present in the moment. They shared stories of times when they had felt deeply connected to others and talked about the ways in which they had built those relationships. Sarah listened intently, taking in every word and feeling a sense of belonging she had never experienced before.

Over the next few weeks, Sarah attended the group's meetings regularly, and with each passing session, she felt more and more connected to the people around her. She shared her own stories and vulnerabilities, and the group listened with empathy and understanding. As the weeks went by, she found herself feeling more confident and open to forming new relationships.

The group also encouraged her to take intentional steps towards building relationships with the people around her. They suggested she join a club or volunteer in her community, and Sarah followed their advice. She started volunteering at a local shelter and joined a book club, and before she knew it, she had formed a network of friends and acquaintances who shared her values and passions.

As she looked back on her journey, Sarah realized that

intentional relationships were not about finding the perfect person, but about creating a space for meaningful connections to flourish. She was grateful for the garden and the community she had found there, and she knew that she would always carry the lessons she had learned with her on her journey towards deeper connection and authenticity.

70

The Mountain of Empowered Boundaries: Saying No with Grace and Assertiveness.

Once upon a time, there was a young woman named Lily who struggled with setting boundaries. She often found herself saying yes to things she didn't want to do, simply to please others. She would end up feeling drained, resentful, and unable to focus on her own priorities.

One day, Lily went for a hike in the mountains. She found herself on a steep and rocky trail, feeling uncertain about whether she could make it to the top. But with each step, she felt more and more empowered, her muscles growing stronger and her breathing steadier.

As she climbed higher, Lily thought about the parallels between climbing a mountain and setting boundaries. Both require effort and determination, but both also lead to a greater sense of strength and self-confidence.

Finally, Lily reached the top of the mountain, where she was rewarded with a breathtaking view. As she looked out over the landscape, she felt a sense of peace and clarity wash over her.

In that moment, she made a decision to start setting boundaries in her life. She knew it wouldn't be easy, but she was determined to do it with grace and assertiveness.

Over the coming weeks and months, Lily practiced saying no to things that didn't align with her values or goals. She communicated her needs and boundaries clearly and kindly, even when it was uncomfortable.

To her surprise, her relationships improved as a result. She felt more respected and valued by her friends and family, and she was able to focus on the things that truly mattered to her.

Lily realized that setting boundaries wasn't about being selfish or uncaring. It was about respecting herself and others, and creating a healthier and more fulfilling life for everyone involved.

As she looked out at the mountain range once again, Lily felt a deep sense of gratitude for the lessons she had learned. She knew that there would be more challenges and setbacks along the way, but she felt confident that she could face them with grace and assertiveness, just like she had on this mountain.

71

The Garden of Inner Peace: Finding Calm Amidst the Chaos

In a small village nestled in the mountains, there lived a young woman named Mei. She was known in the village for her kindness and willingness to help others. Despite living a simple life, Mei was always content and at peace with herself. Her secret? She had found her garden of inner peace.

One day, Mei's village was hit by a sudden storm that destroyed many homes and crops. Everyone in the village was in distress, but Mei remained calm and composed. She gathered a few of her friends and started helping the families whose homes were damaged. They provided shelter, food, and clothing to those in need.

As they were working, Mei's friends couldn't help but ask her how she managed to remain so calm and focused in the midst of such chaos. Mei simply smiled and said, "I have found my garden of inner peace."

Curious, her friends asked her to explain what she meant. Mei led them to a small garden behind her house. The garden was surrounded by beautiful flowers, herbs, and trees. In the center of the garden was a small pond with a tranquil fountain. The sound of the water and the fragrance of the flowers had a calming effect on anyone who entered the garden.

Mei shared that whenever she felt overwhelmed or anxious, she would come to her garden and sit by the pond. She would close her eyes and focus on her breath, letting her worries and fears drift away with each exhale. She would visualize herself surrounded by a warm, comforting light, and feel a sense of peace wash over her.

Her friends were amazed at how such a small garden could have such a profound effect on Mei's well-being. Inspired by Mei's example, they decided to create their own gardens of inner peace, each unique to their own personalities and preferences.

From that day on, whenever they faced challenges or difficulties, Mei and her friends would come together in their gardens of inner peace to find solace and strength. The gardens became a symbol of hope and resilience for the village, and many people started creating their own gardens.

Mei had shown that even in the midst of chaos and uncertainty, it is possible to find a sense of calm and peace within ourselves. The garden of inner peace is always within reach, waiting for us to tend to it with mindfulness and care.

72

The Circle of Radical Acceptance: Embracing Life's Imperfections with Love and Compassion

There was once a village nestled in a valley, surrounded by towering mountains. The people of the village were happy and content, going about their daily lives with a sense of ease and simplicity. But one day, a terrible storm rolled in, causing a massive landslide that destroyed many homes and farms, and left the village in ruins.

As the villagers surveyed the damage, many felt overwhelmed with despair and anger. They blamed each other for not being more prepared, and for not working harder to prevent the disaster. But one woman, named Mei, felt a different kind of emotion stirring inside her. She felt a deep sense of acceptance and compassion, for herself and for her fellow villagers.

Mei began to gather her neighbors and friends, and together

they worked tirelessly to rebuild the village. They helped each other clear away the rubble, mend roofs, and plant new crops. They worked long into the night, but their spirits were high, and they felt a newfound sense of community and togetherness.

As they worked, Mei shared her thoughts on radical acceptance with anyone who would listen. She explained that it was okay to feel sad and angry about what had happened, but that it was also important to accept the situation as it was, without blame or judgment. She encouraged everyone to focus on what they could do to make things better, rather than dwelling on what they couldn't change.

Slowly but surely, the village began to thrive again. The crops grew tall and strong, the homes were rebuilt, and the people began to smile and laugh again. Mei's message of radical acceptance had taken root in the hearts of the villagers, and they found a new sense of peace and joy in their lives.

Years went by, and Mei became known as the wise woman of the village. She taught her children and grandchildren the importance of radical acceptance, and they, in turn, passed on her teachings to future generations.

Eventually, when Mei was an old woman, she passed away peacefully in her sleep. The villagers mourned her passing, but they also felt immense gratitude for the lessons she had taught them. They knew that she had left a lasting legacy of love and acceptance, and that her spirit would live on in the hearts of everyone who had known her.

And so, the village continued to flourish, thanks in large part to Mei's message of radical acceptance. The people of the village learned to embrace life's imperfections with love and compassion, and in doing so, they found a deep sense of peace and contentment that would stay with them for generations to come.

73

The Forest of Self-Discovery: Finding Purpose and Passion Through Personal Growth

Once there was a young woman named Maya who felt lost and unsure of her place in the world. She had graduated from college with a degree in business, but after a few years in the corporate world, she realized that it wasn't fulfilling her. She felt like something was missing, but she couldn't quite put her finger on what it was.

One day, Maya decided to take a solo camping trip in the forest to clear her head and think about her future. As she wandered through the woods, she stumbled upon an old, abandoned cabin. The door was slightly ajar, and she couldn't resist the urge to peek inside.

To her surprise, the cabin was filled with old books, journals, and maps. Maya felt drawn to them and spent hours reading about the history of the forest and the adventures of its previous inhabitants. As she read, she felt a sense of excitement and wonder that she hadn't felt in years.

The next day, Maya set out on a hike to explore the forest further. She followed a trail that led her to a beautiful clearing filled with wildflowers and tall trees. In the center of the clearing was a large rock with a message carved into it: "Find your passion, and you will find your purpose."

Maya sat down on the rock and closed her eyes. She took a deep breath and let her thoughts wander. Suddenly, she had a vision of herself teaching a group of children about nature and the environment. The idea filled her with joy, and she knew that it was her true calling.

Maya returned home from her trip with a newfound sense of purpose. She quit her job and enrolled in a program to become an environmental educator. She started volunteering at local parks and nature centers and eventually landed a job teaching children about the importance of conservation.

As she watched the children's faces light up with wonder and excitement, Maya knew that she had found her true calling. The forest had shown her the way to self-discovery and had helped her find her passion and purpose in life.

From that day on, Maya continued to explore the forest and its secrets. She discovered that the forest was full of surprises and that there was always something new to learn. Maya never forgot the lesson that the forest had taught her: to follow her heart and trust that the path would lead her where she was meant to be.

74

The Bridge of Empathetic Listening: Understanding Others Through Active Listening and Empathy

Once upon a time, in a small village nestled between two hills, there lived a wise man known for his empathetic listening. People from all over the village would come to him with their problems, seeking his guidance and advice.

One day, a young woman came to the wise man, seeking his help. She was struggling with a difficult situation in her family, where her parents were going through a rough patch in their marriage. She felt torn between her loyalty towards both her parents and didn't know what to do.

The wise man listened to her patiently, nodding and asking questions to understand her situation better. He could sense the turmoil within her and knew that she needed his empathy more than his advice.

After a while, he spoke, "I can see how difficult this is for you. It must be tough to see your parents going through a difficult time. You must be feeling like you're caught in the middle. It takes a lot of strength to handle a situation like this, and I know you have that strength within you."

The young woman was taken aback by his response. She had expected him to tell her what to do or give her some advice on how to handle the situation. But the wise man's response made her feel understood and heard.

He continued, "It's essential to remember that you're not responsible for your parents' happiness or their problems. It's okay to feel torn and confused. Just remember to be kind to yourself and to both your parents. You can be there for them without taking sides. It's not an easy thing to do, but I know you have it in you."

The young woman left the wise man's home feeling a sense of peace and calm that she hadn't felt in a long time. She realized that sometimes, all we need is someone to listen to us and understand our situation without judgment or advice.

From that day on, the young woman started practicing empathetic listening with her family and friends. She realized that being present for someone and offering them empathy and support is sometimes more valuable than giving them advice.

The wise man's lesson stayed with her throughout her life, and she became known in her village for her empathetic listening skills. She helped many people in her community, just as the wise man had helped her.

In conclusion, the story teaches us the importance of empathetic listening and understanding others. Often, we are too quick to give advice or judge others without understanding their situation. But if we can take a moment to listen to them and offer them empathy, we can make a significant difference in their lives.

75

The Path of Mindful Healing: Nurturing Your Body and Soul Through Self-Care and Mindfulness

Sophie had always been the caretaker in her family. She looked after her younger siblings, helped her parents with their chores, and even supported her grandparents when they needed help. Despite her busy schedule, Sophie always put her family's needs before her own.

But one day, Sophie realized that she couldn't continue to neglect her own needs. She had been experiencing stress and anxiety, and her body was showing signs of exhaustion. She knew she needed to make a change and focus on her own self-care.

Sophie began to prioritize her mental and physical health. She started meditating every morning, going for walks in nature, and practicing yoga. She also began to pay attention to her diet, eating healthy foods that nourished her body and mind.

As Sophie began to heal and care for herself, she noticed a significant change in her relationships with her family. She was more patient, understanding, and empathetic. She was able to communicate her needs clearly and set healthy boundaries with her loved ones.

One day, Sophie's younger sister came to her in tears, feeling overwhelmed and stressed. Sophie listened attentively and empathetically, offering her sister comfort and support. She suggested that they practice yoga together and offered to make her sister a healthy meal. Her sister was grateful and relieved, and Sophie felt empowered by her ability to provide support while also caring for herself.

Sophie's journey to mindful healing had not only transformed her own life but had also positively impacted those around her. She had learned that self-care was not selfish, but essential to being able to show up as her best self for others.

As Sophie continued on her path of mindful healing, she inspired those around her to prioritize their own self-care. She became a role model for her family, showing them that taking care of themselves was not only beneficial to their own well-being but also strengthened their relationships with one another.

Sophie realized that by focusing on her own self-care, she was able to give more to others from a place of abundance and love. She had discovered the power of mindful healing, and she knew that it was a lifelong journey worth continuing.

76

The Ocean of Abundant Joy: Cultivating Happiness and Gratitude in Everyday Life

I n a small coastal village, there was a fisherman named Miguel who lived a simple life. He fished every day and provided for his family, but he always felt like something was missing. He noticed that the other villagers always seemed so happy and joyful, even though they had less than he did. Miguel couldn't understand it.

One day, Miguel decided to ask the village elder, a wise old woman named Maria, how the other villagers could be so happy with so little. Maria smiled at him and said, "Miguel, happiness is not about what you have, but about what you appreciate. Come with me."

Maria took Miguel on a walk along the beach and pointed to the vast ocean before them. "Look at the ocean, Miguel. It's vast and beautiful, and it brings us so much joy. But it's not just the ocean that brings us joy; it's the way we appreciate it. We don't just see the ocean; we feel it. We let its beauty wash over us and fill us with gratitude. That's the key to joy."

Miguel didn't fully understand Maria's words, but he was determined to try. The next day, as he went out to fish, he made a point of appreciating the ocean. He noticed the way the sun sparkled on the waves, the sound of the seagulls, and the feel of the salty breeze on his skin. As he fished, he let his gratitude for the ocean fill his heart.

As the days went on, Miguel began to see the world in a new way. He started to appreciate the little things, like the laughter of his children, the smell of fresh-baked bread, and the sound of rain tapping on his roof. He felt a sense of joy he had never felt before.

One day, while fishing, Miguel noticed a group of tourists on the beach, taking pictures of the ocean. He walked over to them and said, "Excuse me, I'm Miguel. I'm a fisherman here. I noticed you taking pictures of the ocean, but I wanted to tell you that the real beauty of the ocean is not just in its appearance. It's in the way it makes you feel. Take a moment to appreciate it with all your senses, and I promise you'll feel a sense of joy like you've never felt before."

The tourists looked at Miguel skeptically, but they decided to try it. They closed their eyes and listened to the waves, felt the sun on their faces, and let the beauty of the ocean wash over them. When they opened their eyes, they were surprised to find tears in their eyes. They thanked Miguel for his wisdom and went on their way.

Miguel returned to his fishing with a sense of joy and purpose. He realized that life was not about what you had, but about how you appreciated it. From that day on, he lived every day with gratitude and joy in his heart, and he knew he would never go back to the way he used to be.

77

The Mountain of Fearless Exploration: Stepping Out of Your Comfort Zone and Embracing New Experiences

Once there was a young woman named Mia who had always lived a sheltered life. She was content in her routines and familiar surroundings, never venturing far from what she knew. But deep down, she felt a longing for something more. She wanted to see the world and experience all the beauty and adventure it had to offer.

One day, she decided to take a bold step and book a trip to a remote mountain range she had always been curious about. She was nervous, but also excited to challenge herself and step out of her comfort zone.

As she began her ascent up the steep mountain trail, she felt a sense of awe and wonder at the breathtaking scenery around her. The air was crisp and fresh, and the towering peaks loomed majestically in the distance. She pushed herself harder than she ever had before, her legs burning with each step, but she was determined to reach the summit.

Despite some setbacks and moments of doubt along the way, Mia persevered and finally made it to the top. The view was even more spectacular than she had imagined, and she felt a surge of pride and accomplishment. As she sat and gazed out at the vast expanse before her, she realized that this was only the beginning. There was still so much more to explore and discover.

Mia's journey up the mountain had taught her an important lesson about fear and taking risks. She had been afraid of the unknown, of stepping out of her comfort zone, but the reward for her bravery had been an experience that filled her with wonder and joy.

From that moment on, Mia decided to approach life with the same fearlessness and determination she had shown on the mountain. She knew that there would be challenges and setbacks along the way, but she was ready to face them head-on and keep exploring the endless possibilities that awaited her.

As she made her way down the mountain, Mia felt a sense of liberation and gratitude for the adventure she had just undertaken. She knew that she would carry this experience with her for the rest of her life, a reminder to always push herself beyond her limits and never be afraid to explore the unknown.

78

The Circle of Resilient Optimism: Choosing Positivity and Hope in the Face of Adversity

O nce upon a time, there was a young woman named Maya who had just graduated from college. She had always been an optimistic person, seeing the best in every situation and spreading positivity wherever she went. However, things didn't go as planned after she graduated. She couldn't find a job in her field, and the pandemic made the job market even tougher. Maya was feeling hopeless and defeated.

One day, Maya decided to take a hike up a nearby mountain. As she climbed higher and higher, the air became thinner and the climb more difficult. But with each step, she felt a sense of accomplishment and pride. She finally reached the top and looked out at the breathtaking view of the valley below. Maya realized that just like the climb up the mountain, life is full of challenges, but it's up to us to keep pushing forward and not give up.

As she made her way back down the mountain, Maya thought about her situation and decided to take a more positive outlook. She started volunteering at a local non-profit, which helped her gain experience and meet new people. Maya also reached out to her network and was able to secure a part-time job that eventually led to a full-time position in her field.

Through the challenges, Maya learned the power of resilience and optimism. She started a group on social media to spread positivity and inspire others to keep going, even when things get tough. Maya's journey up the mountain reminded her that life is full of ups and downs, but by choosing to focus on the positives and maintaining a hopeful outlook, we can overcome any obstacle that comes our way.

From then on, Maya made a conscious effort to choose resilience and optimism in every situation. She faced new challenges head-on, always keeping in mind that just like her climb up the mountain, there would be difficulties, but with the right mindset, she could overcome them.

Maya's story is a reminder that life is full of obstacles, but we can choose how we react to them. By maintaining a positive outlook and staying resilient, we can overcome anything and achieve our dreams.

79

The Garden of Authentic Expression: Honoring Your Truth and Sharing Your Voice with Confidence

In the Garden of Authentic Expression, a young woman named Lily tended to her garden of flowers and herbs with great care. She had always loved the way that plants could grow and flourish under the right conditions, and she felt a kinship with them.

One day, as Lily was weeding her garden, she noticed a tiny sprout that had just broken through the soil. It was a small, delicate thing, but she could sense its potential for growth and beauty.

As the days passed, Lily watched the sprout grow into a sturdy stem with leaves and buds. She marveled at the way it seemed to stretch toward the sun, reaching higher and higher with each passing day.

One morning, Lily woke up to find that the bud on the stem had bloomed into a vibrant, colorful flower. It was a sight to behold, and she felt a sense of pride and joy knowing that she had played a part in its growth.

As she admired the flower, she realized that it was a metaphor for her own journey of self-expression. Just like the flower, she had the potential to bloom and thrive if she nurtured herself and stayed true to her authentic self.

For years, Lily had struggled to speak up for herself and share her thoughts and feelings with others. She had always been afraid of being judged or rejected, so she had kept her true self hidden away.

But as she watched the flower in her garden, she realized that hiding her true self was like keeping a seed in the dark. It might be safe, but it would never grow and blossom into something beautiful.

So, Lily made a decision to start speaking her truth, even if it felt uncomfortable or scary. She started small, sharing her opinions with friends and family, and gradually worked up the courage to express herself more boldly.

It wasn't always easy, but every time she spoke her truth, she felt a sense of liberation and empowerment. She realized that her authentic expression was like sunlight for her soul, nourishing her and helping her grow into her fullest potential.

In the Garden of Authentic Expression, Lily learned that

staying true to herself was the key to unlocking her inner beauty and radiance. And just like the flower in her garden, she bloomed and flourished in ways she had never imagined possible.

The River of Mindful Creativity: Tapping into Your Creative Flow to Find Inspiration and Fulfillment

In a small town nestled in the mountains, there lived a young woman named Lily. She was a shy and reserved person, always keeping to herself and afraid to speak her mind. Lily had always loved writing and creating stories, but she never shared them with anyone, fearing judgment and rejection.

One day, as Lily was walking by the river that ran through the town, she saw a group of children playing and laughing as they splashed in the water. She noticed that they were all wearing handmade bracelets, and she couldn't help but feel curious. She approached them and asked where they got the bracelets. One of the children smiled at her and said, "We made them ourselves! Do you want to join us?"

Lily hesitated for a moment, but then she remembered her love for creating things. She accepted the invitation and spent the afternoon with the children, making bracelets and sharing stories. For the first time in a long time, she felt a sense of joy and fulfillment.

As Lily walked home that day, she felt inspired. She realized that creating things was what made her truly happy, and she didn't want to keep it to herself anymore. She decided to start a blog where she could share her writing and creations with the world.

At first, she was afraid of what people might think of her work, but she remembered the joy she felt when she shared her creations with the children by the river. She wrote her first blog post, pouring her heart and soul into it, and hit the publish button.

Days went by, and Lily received no response. She began to doubt herself and wonder if she had made a mistake. But one day, she received a message from a stranger who had stumbled upon her blog. They told her how much they loved her writing and how it had inspired them to pursue their own creative passions.

Lily was amazed. She realized that by sharing her creativity with the world, she was making a difference in someone's life. She continued to write and create, and her blog began to gain more and more followers.

Lily had found her place in the world, and it was through her creativity. She had discovered the river of mindful creativity, and it had led her to a place of inspiration and fulfillment.

81

The Path of Gracious Humility: Balancing Confidence and Humility to Build Stronger Relationships and Communities

Once upon a time, there was a successful businessman named Jack. Jack was always on the top of his game, and he knew it. He had worked hard to get where he was, and he wasn't afraid to let others know it.

One day, Jack was invited to speak at a business conference. As he prepared his speech, he couldn't help but feel a sense of pride in all of his accomplishments. He was sure that everyone would be impressed by his success and his confidence.

But as Jack took the stage, he realized that something was off. The audience seemed restless and disinterested, and Jack's words seemed to fall flat.

Feeling embarrassed and frustrated, Jack finished his speech and quickly left the stage. He couldn't shake the feeling that he had done something wrong, but he didn't know what it was.

As he thought about the experience, Jack realized that his confidence had become arrogance. He had been so focused on his own success that he had forgotten about the importance of humility and empathy. He had failed to connect with his audience because he had been too busy talking about himself.

Determined to make things right, Jack started to practice gracious humility. He began to listen more than he spoke, and he made an effort to understand other people's perspectives. He apologized for his previous behavior and worked hard to build stronger relationships with his colleagues and employees.

As time went on, Jack's efforts paid off. He found that he was able to connect with people on a deeper level, and he started to see the world through a new lens. He realized that his success wasn't just about him - it was about the people who had supported him along the way.

Through his experience, Jack learned that humility and confidence are not mutually exclusive. In fact, they work together to create a strong and supportive community. And in the end, it was this community that helped Jack achieve even greater success than he ever could have imagined.

82

The Ocean of Endless Possibilities: Embracing Uncertainty and Taking Risks

There was a young woman named Maya who had always played it safe. She was content with her routine job and comfortable life, but deep down, she felt a sense of restlessness. She yearned for something more, something that would make her heart beat faster and give her life meaning.

One day, Maya decided to take a chance and sign up for a surfing lesson. She had always been fascinated by the ocean and the thrill of riding waves, but she had never tried it herself. As she stood on the beach, looking out at the vast expanse of water before her, she felt a mixture of excitement and fear.

The instructor showed Maya the basics of surfing, but it wasn't easy. She fell off her board countless times, swallowing

221

saltwater and feeling frustrated. But with each attempt, she learned a little more and got a little closer to catching a wave.

Finally, after what felt like hours of trying, Maya felt the board lift beneath her and the rush of the wave propelling her forward. She rode it all the way to the shore, whooping with joy and feeling more alive than she had in years.

From that day on, Maya was hooked. She began to take surfing lessons regularly, pushing herself to improve and try new things. She found that the ocean was a place of endless possibility, where she could challenge herself and discover new strengths she never knew she had.

As she continued to surf, Maya's life began to change in unexpected ways. She found herself taking risks she never would have considered before, speaking up in meetings at work and taking on new projects. She felt more confident in herself and her abilities, and her relationships with friends and family deepened as she opened herself up to new experiences.

Looking back, Maya realized that her fear of uncertainty had held her back for too long. By embracing the unknown and taking risks, she had discovered a sense of freedom and possibility that had been missing from her life. She knew that there would always be challenges ahead, but she felt ready to face them head-on, with the courage and resilience that came from riding the waves.

83

The Mountain of Radical Self-Love: Honoring Yourself and Your Boundaries

At the foot of the Mountain of Radical Self-Love, there lived a woman named Maya. Maya was a kind, compassionate person who always put the needs of others before her own. She had a heart of gold and went out of her way to help those in need. However, Maya struggled with loving herself and often neglected her own needs.

One day, Maya decided to climb the Mountain of Radical Self-Love. As she climbed higher and higher, she noticed the breathtaking views around her. She saw the beauty in the world and realized that she, too, was part of that beauty.

As she climbed higher, the air became thinner, and the climb became more difficult. Maya began to doubt herself, wondering if she was strong enough to make it to the top.

But with each step, she reminded herself of the love and compassion she gave to others, and she knew she deserved that same love and compassion from herself.

Maya reached the summit of the mountain and saw a beautiful garden filled with flowers of all colors. In the center of the garden was a mirror. Maya approached the mirror and saw her reflection for the first time in a long time. She saw the lines on her face, the scars on her body, and the imperfections she had always tried to hide. But this time, she didn't feel shame or disgust. Instead, she saw a strong, resilient woman who had overcome many obstacles.

Maya realized that true self-love meant accepting herself, flaws and all. She made a promise to herself to always honor her boundaries, to take care of herself, and to love herself unconditionally.

As she descended the mountain, Maya felt lighter and happier. She no longer felt burdened by the weight of self-doubt and insecurity. Maya knew that she had a long way to go on her journey of self-love, but she also knew that she was strong enough to face any challenge.

Maya returned to her village with a newfound confidence and joy. She continued to help others, but this time, she did so while also taking care of herself. And whenever she felt doubt creeping in, she thought of the beautiful garden and the mirror on the Mountain of Radical Self-Love, and she was reminded of her own strength and worth.

84

The Garden of Compassionate Communication: Building Bridges Through Understanding and Empathy

Once upon a time, there was a community of people who lived in a beautiful garden filled with vibrant flowers, tall trees, and meandering paths. The garden was a peaceful place where everyone was happy, but sometimes misunderstandings would arise, and conflicts would occur.

One day, a wise woman arrived in the garden, and she noticed that the people there were having trouble communicating with one another. She decided to teach them a lesson about the importance of compassionate communication.

The wise woman called everyone to gather around her and began to tell them a story. She spoke of a time when she was young and had a disagreement with her best friend. They both felt hurt and angry, and for a while, they stopped speaking to each other. But then, they decided to sit down and talk things out.

The wise woman explained that when we communicate with compassion, we can listen and understand each other's perspectives. We can avoid judging and blaming and instead focus on finding a solution that works for everyone. She encouraged the people in the garden to practice active listening and to express themselves clearly and respectfully.

The community took the wise woman's words to heart, and they began to work on their communication skills. They learned to approach each other with empathy and to ask open-ended questions to gain a better understanding of each other's needs and desires. They also learned to be patient and to take the time to truly listen to what others had to say.

As they practiced compassionate communication, they found that their relationships with one another grew stronger. They were able to resolve conflicts more quickly and easily, and they felt a deeper sense of connection and understanding with one another.

The garden became a place of harmony and cooperation, where everyone felt valued and heard. And the wise woman, who had taught them the importance of compassionate communication, smiled and knew that she had helped create something truly special.

From that day on, the people in the garden made it a point to practice compassionate communication in all their interactions, and they lived happily ever after, in a garden filled with beautiful flowers and even more beautiful relationships.

85

The Path of Intentional Living: Creating a Life of Meaning and Purpose

As soon as she woke up, Marie knew it was going to be a great day. She jumped out of bed, excited to start her new journey towards intentional living. For years, Marie had been going through the motions of life, just going where the wind took her. But now, she was determined to take control of her life and live with intention.

Marie had always been drawn to helping others, so she decided to start by volunteering at her local community center. She spent her days tutoring children and helping with community events. She found that helping others gave her a sense of purpose and fulfillment that she had never experienced before.

As she became more intentional in her actions, Marie began to notice a shift in her relationships. She started to focus on the people who brought positivity and joy into her life, and let go of the toxic relationships that had been holding her back. This allowed her to cultivate deeper connections with those who truly cared for her.

Marie also started to take better care of her physical and mental health. She began to make time for exercise and meditation, and started eating healthier foods. She found that when she took care of her body, her mind was more clear and focused.

One day, while volunteering at the community center, Marie met a woman named Sarah. Sarah was a single mother who was struggling to make ends meet. Marie felt a strong connection to Sarah and decided to help her in any way she could. She started by offering to babysit Sarah's children while she worked. Over time, Marie and Sarah became close friends, and Marie became like a second mother to Sarah's children.

Through intentional living, Marie had found a new sense of purpose and fulfillment. She was helping others, taking care of herself, and cultivating deeper relationships. She felt truly alive for the first time in years.

Marie's intentional living had a ripple effect on those around her. She inspired others to live with intention and purpose, and her positive energy was contagious. People in her community started to come together, and they worked together to make their community a better place.

Marie realized that intentional living wasn't just about making her own life better, but it was about creating a better world for everyone. And with that realization, she knew that she would continue on her path of intentional living, with a heart full of gratitude and a commitment to making a difference in the world.

86

The Circle of Resilient Connection: Navigating Loneliness and Building Meaningful Relationships

In a bustling city, there lived a woman named Sophia who had always been surrounded by people, yet felt lonely deep down. She had a lot of acquaintances, but no real friends or connections. Her busy work life left little time for socializing, and she often found herself scrolling through social media feeds, envious of others who seemed to have thriving social lives.

One day, she decided enough was enough. She realized that the problem was not with others, but with herself. She needed to work on building real connections with people, rather than just superficial relationships. She set out on a journey to find ways to connect with others and build meaningful relationships.

She started by joining a local volunteering group. Here, she met people who were passionate about making a difference in their community. She felt a sense of belonging and found that working together for a common cause brought people closer.

Next, she started attending a weekly meditation class. Through this practice, she learned to connect with her inner self and gain clarity on her values and priorities. She found that when she was clear about her own needs and values, it was easier to build meaningful connections with others.

Sophia also started attending a book club where she met people who shared her love for literature. Through the discussions and debates, she discovered new perspectives and insights, which helped her grow as a person.

As she started building more connections, Sophia realized that it was not just about finding people who were similar to her, but also about embracing diversity and different perspectives. She started attending cultural events and festivals, trying new foods, and learning about different cultures.

In time, Sophia had built a community of diverse and mean-ingful connections. She no longer felt lonely, as she had people in her life who shared her values and interests. She learned that building meaningful relationships required effort and vulnerability, but the rewards were worth it.

Sophia realized that loneliness is not just about being physi-cally alone, but about feeling disconnected from others. She had found her way out of loneliness by building resilient connections with others. She knew that it was an ongoing process, but with the right mindset and actions, she could continue to build strong relationships and create a life of meaningful connections.

The Forest of Mindful Self-Compassion: Embracing Your Imperfections with Kindness

Once upon a time, there was a forest where all the trees were different, some tall and strong, others small and delicate, but each one had its unique beauty. However, there was a tree that was different from all the others. It was a tall and mighty oak tree, the oldest and most respected tree in the forest. The animals would gather around the oak tree to listen to its wisdom and guidance.

One day, a little sapling approached the oak tree, feeling insecure and insignificant compared to the grandeur of the oak tree. The oak tree could sense the sapling's unease and asked, "Why do you look so worried, little one?"

"I feel so small and insignificant compared to you, the grand oak tree," the sapling said, feeling ashamed of its small size.

The oak tree smiled kindly and said, "My dear, you may be small now, but you have the potential to grow tall and strong like me. It takes time and patience, but with nurturing and care, you can reach great heights."

The sapling felt a glimmer of hope and asked, "But what if I am not as beautiful or as grand as you?"

The oak tree replied, "My dear, beauty is not measured by size or grandeur. You are unique in your own way, and that is what makes you beautiful. Embrace your imperfections, and they will become your strengths."

With those words of wisdom, the little sapling began to grow, reaching towards the sky with each passing day. It learned to embrace its imperfections, the twists and turns of its branches, and the scars that told its story. And as it grew, it became a source of inspiration for other saplings in the forest, who also learned to embrace their uniqueness and grow towards their full potential.

The oak tree continued to watch over the sapling, nurturing and guiding it along the way. And as the years passed, the sapling grew tall and strong, becoming a beautiful tree in its own right.

In the end, the sapling learned that self-compassion and self-acceptance were the keys to reaching its full potential. It learned that it was not about being like the grand oak tree or any other tree in the forest but about embracing its unique qualities and growing towards its own destiny.

The forest was filled with trees of all shapes and sizes, each with its unique beauty. And the little sapling, now a mighty tree, stood tall and proud, grateful for the oak tree's guidance and the lessons it had learned along the way.

88

The Bridge of Forgiveness and Reconciliation: Finding Healing and Closure Through Letting Go of Resentment

In a small village, there lived two friends, Ravi and Suresh. They had been the best of friends since their childhood, playing together, studying together, and even working together in the same field. They were like two peas in a pod until one day, they had a massive argument, and their friendship came to an abrupt end.

Both of them felt hurt and betrayed, and neither of them was ready to apologize. The tension between them grew, and they started avoiding each other. It became difficult for the people around them to see two good friends become enemies.

One day, Ravi realized that he missed his friend dearly and decided to make amends. He went to Suresh's house and apologized for his behavior. To Ravi's surprise, Suresh not only accepted his apology but also apologized for his part in the argument. They hugged each other, and their friendship was rekindled.

Ravi and Suresh realized that their friendship was worth more than their ego and anger. They understood that holding onto resentment and anger would only lead to pain and suffering. They decided to forgive each other and move on.

Their friendship became stronger than ever before, and they learned the true meaning of forgiveness and reconciliation. They started talking about their issues and misunderstandings and resolved them before they could turn into arguments.

Their story of forgiveness and reconciliation spread through the village, inspiring many to let go of their grudges and forgive those who had wronged them. They learned that forgiveness was not just about letting go of the past, but it was also about freeing oneself from the burden of resentment and anger.

Ravi and Suresh became a bridge of forgiveness and reconciliation for their village, and their act of forgiveness brought healing and closure to many broken relationships.

Their story reminds us that forgiveness is not a sign of weakness, but it is a powerful act of courage and strength. It takes a lot of courage to let go of the hurt and anger, but it is worth it in the end. Forgiveness is not about forgetting the past, but it is about moving forward with love, understanding, and compassion.

89

The River of Abundant Creativity: Unleashing Your Creative Potential to Enrich Your Life and Others

Once upon a time, in a small town nestled beside a winding river, there lived a young woman named Lila. Lila was a talented artist, but she struggled to find inspiration for her work. She spent long hours staring at blank canvases, feeling frustrated and lost.

One day, as Lila sat by the riverbank, she watched the water flow by, glistening in the sunlight. Suddenly, an idea struck her, and she rushed back to her studio to put it into action. She spent hours working on her painting, letting the colors and shapes flow out of her with ease.

As she stepped back to admire her work, Lila realized that the key to unlocking her creativity had been right in front of her all along. The river had reminded her that creativity, like water, cannot be forced or controlled. It must be allowed to flow freely and take its own natural course.

With this newfound insight, Lila began to approach her art with a sense of playfulness and curiosity. She explored new techniques, experimented with different mediums, and let her intuition guide her. And with each stroke of her brush, she felt a sense of joy and fulfillment that had been missing from her work before.

As Lila's art began to gain recognition and praise, she realized that her journey had not just been about discovering her own creativity, but also about inspiring others to do the same. She started holding workshops and classes, encouraging people to tap into their own creative potential and let go of self-doubt and perfectionism.

Years went by, and Lila continued to create and teach. She watched as her students blossomed into confident artists and found new meaning and purpose in their lives. And as she sat by the river, watching the water flow by, she knew that she had found her true calling – to help others unleash the abundant creativity that lay within them.

The lesson that Lila learned was simple yet profound – that creativity is not something to be forced or controlled, but rather something to be allowed to flow freely and take its own course. When we let go of our expectations and allow ourselves to play and explore, we can tap into a wellspring of inspiration and joy that enriches our lives and the lives of those around us.

90

The Garden of Authentic Gratitude: Cultivating a Grateful Heart and Appreciating Life's Beauty

I n a small village nestled in the heart of the countryside, there lived a young girl named Maya. She was known for her positive attitude and her infectious smile, which could brighten up even the gloomiest of days. Maya's family had always instilled in her the importance of gratitude and appreciation for the simple things in life. As a result, she had developed a deep sense of appreciation for the beauty around her, whether it was the vibrant colors of the flowers in the garden or the sweet sound of the birds singing in the morning.

One day, while walking through the village, Maya stumbled upon an elderly woman who was struggling to carry a heavy basket of groceries. Without hesitation, Maya offered to help the woman, and together they made their way back to the woman's small cottage. As they approached the cottage, Maya couldn't help but notice the stunning garden that surrounded it. The flowers were arranged in beautiful patterns, and the colors were so vibrant that they seemed to glow in the sunlight.

The elderly woman noticed Maya's admiration for her garden and invited her to take a closer look. As they walked through the garden, the woman pointed out each flower and shared its unique story. Maya was captivated by the woman's passion and love for her garden, and she felt a deep sense of gratitude for the opportunity to experience its beauty.

From that day on, Maya made a habit of visiting the woman's garden regularly. She learned everything she could about the different types of flowers and plants and even started her own small garden at home. Whenever she felt overwhelmed or stressed, she would spend time tending to her garden, and she found that it brought her a sense of peace and calm.

Over time, Maya began to notice a change in herself. She became more patient and compassionate towards others, and she started to appreciate the small things in life even more. She realized that gratitude was not just a feeling but a way of life, and she was grateful for the lessons she had learned from the woman's garden.

Years later, when Maya had grown old, she passed on her love of gardening to her grandchildren. She would tell them stories of the beautiful garden she had discovered in her youth and teach them the importance of gratitude and appreciation. Maya may have passed away, but her legacy lived on through her family and the generations that followed.

The Garden of Authentic Gratitude teaches us to appreciate the beauty in our lives and the world around us. It reminds us that even the smallest things can bring us joy and that gratitude can transform our outlook on life.

91

The Path of Mindful Leadership: Inspiring and Empowering Others Through Conscious Action and Integrity

I n a small village nestled in the mountains, there lived a humble and kind-hearted man named Arun. Arun was the leader of his community, and he was beloved by all. His leadership style was unique in that he always led with compassion and mindfulness.

One day, Arun received a message from the neighboring village that there had been a dispute over land rights. The villagers were frustrated and angry, and they were on the brink of conflict. Arun knew that he had to act quickly to prevent violence from erupting.

He called a meeting with the leaders of the neighboring village and listened to their concerns with an open mind and heart.

He empathized with their frustrations and acknowledged the validity of their grievances. Arun also shared his own perspective and worked with them to find a mutually beneficial solution.

Arun's approach was not to overpower the other village, but to build a bridge of understanding and cooperation. He made sure that everyone felt heard and respected, and he encouraged the villagers to work together towards a common goal.With Arun's leadership, the two villages were able to reach a peaceful resolution. There was no violence, no hatred, and no bitterness. Instead, there was mutual respect, understanding, and a sense of community.

Word of Arun's leadership style spread quickly, and soon, he was invited to speak at leadership conferences and events all over the country. Arun never forgot his roots, and he always made sure to share his experiences with his fellow villagers.

He encouraged them to lead with compassion, mindfulness, and integrity. He reminded them that leadership was not about power, but about service to others. He taught them that true leadership came from the heart and that it was essential to listen to others and to work collaboratively towards common goals.

Years passed, and Arun grew old. He watched with pride as the next generation of leaders emerged from his community. They too were committed to leading with compassion, mindfulness, and integrity. They continued to build bridges of understanding and cooperation, and the village thrived under their leadership.

Arun passed away peacefully, knowing that his legacy would live on. He had shown his community the path of mindful leadership, and they had embraced it wholeheartedly. His village, once a small and isolated community, had become a shining example of what could be achieved through conscious action and integrity.

92

Conclusion & Free Gift

As we come to the end of "Wisdom For The Journey: 100 Inspirational Short Stories For Adults", I hope that these tales have served as a source of inspiration and guidance for you.

Each story in this collection was carefully chosen to offer a unique perspective on the human experience and to remind us all that, no matter where we are on our journeys, we are never alone.

Through the pages of this book, you have been introduced to characters and situations that may have resonated with you on a personal level.

Some stories may have made you laugh, while others may have brought tears to your eyes.

But through it all, I hope that you have been reminded of the beauty and wonder that surrounds us every day.

Remember, life is a journey, and we are all on this path together.

With each step we take, we have the opportunity to learn, grow, and become the best versions of ourselves.

And with each story in this book, you have been given the tools and inspiration to do just that.

So as you close this book and continue on your journey, know that you are capable of great things. Take the wisdom you have gained from these stories and apply it to your own life.

And never forget that the journey is the destination, so make the most of every moment and embrace the adventure that lies ahead.

As for the gift, we want to give you an exclusive invite to check out our Youtube Channel where you will find more riddles for you to enjoy!

Comment on one of the videos if you came from this book! □

Positive reviews from wonderful customers like you help other book enjoyers feel confident about choosing to get this book too.

Sharing your happy experience will be greatly appreciated!